AGAIN THE RINGER

AGAIN THE RINGER

EDGAR WALLACE

WILDSIDE PRESS

TO
MY GENIAL AND BRILLIANT
FRIEND

WALTER HACKETT

Originally published in 1929.

Chapter 1

The Man With The Red Beard

To the average reader the name of Miska Guild is associated with slight and possibly amusing eccentricities. For example, he once went down Regent Street at eleven o'clock at night at sixty miles an hour, crippled two unfortunate pedestrians, and smashed a lamp standard and his car. The charge that he was drunk failed, because indisputably he was sober when he was dragged out of the wreckage, himself unhurt.

Nevertheless, an unsympathetic magistrate convicted, despite the conflict of medical evidence. Miska Guild went to the Sessions with the best advocates that money could buy and had the conviction quashed.

The inner theatrical set knew him as a giver of freakish dinner parties; had an idea that he gave other parties even more freakish but less descriptive. Once he went to Paris, and the French police most obligingly hushed up a lurid incident as best they could.

They could not quite hush up the death of the pretty chorus-girl who was found on the pavement outside the hotel, having fallen from a fifth-floor window, but they were very helpful in explaining that she had mistaken the French windows for the door of her sitting-room. Nobody at the inquiry asked how she managed to climb the balcony.

The only person who evinced a passionate interest in the proceedings was one Henry Arthur Milton, a fugitive from justice, who was staying at the hotel—not as Henry Arthur Milton, certainly not as "The Ringer," by which title he was known; indeed, he bore no name by which the English police could identify him as the best-wanted man in Europe.

Mr. Guild paid heavily for all the trouble he had caused divers police officials and came back to London and to his magnificent flat in Carlton House Terrace quite unabashed, even though some of the theatrical celebrities with whom he was acquainted cut him dead whenever they met him; even though the most unpleasant rumours surrounded his Paris trip.

He was a man of thirty, reputedly a millionaire three times over. It is certain that he was very rich, and had the queerest ideas about what was and what was not the most amusing method of passing time. Had the Paris incident occurred in London neither his two nor his three millions would have availed him, nor all the advocacy of the greatest lawyers averted the most unpleasant consequences.

* * * *

One bright November morning, when the sun rose in a clear blue sky and the leafless trees of Green Park had a peculiar splendour of their own, the second footman brought his breakfast to his bedside, and on the tray there was a registered letter. The postmark was Paris, the envelope was marked "Urgent and confidential; not to be opened by the secretary."

Miska Guild sat up in bed, pushed back his long, yellowish hair from his eyes, bleared for a moment at the envelope and tore it open with a groan. There was a single sheet of paper, closely typewritten. It bore no address and began without a conventional preamble:

> On October 18 you went to Paris, accompanied by a small party. In that party was a girl called Ethel Seddings, who was quite unaware of your character. She committed suicide in order to escape from you. I am called The Ringer; my name is Henry Arthur Milton, and Scotland Yard will furnish you with particulars of my past. As you are a man of considerable property and may wish to have time to make arrangements as to its disposal, I will give you a little grace. At the end of a reasonable period I shall come to London and kill you.

That was all the letter contained. Miska read it through; looked at the back of the sheet for further inspiration; read it through again.

"Who the devil is The Ringer?" he asked.

The footman, who was an authority upon such matters, gave him a little inaccurate information. Miska examined the envelope without being enlightened any further, and then with a chuckle he was about to tear the letter into pieces but thought better of it.

"Send it up to Scotland Yard," he commanded his secretary later in the morning, and would have forgotten the unpleasant communication if he had not returned from lunch to find a rather sinister-looking man with a short black beard who introduced himself as Chief Inspector Bliss from Scotland Yard.

"About that letter? Oh, rot! You're not taking that seriously, are you?"

Bliss nodded slowly.

"So seriously that I'm putting on two of my best men to guard you for a month or two."

Miska looked at him incredulously.

"Do you really mean that? But surely…my footman tells me he's a criminal: he wouldn't dare come to London?"

6

Inspector Bliss smiled grimly.

"He dared go into Scotland Yard when it suited him. This is the kind of case that would interest him."

He recounted a few of The Ringer's earlier cases, and Miska Guild became of a sudden a very agitated young man.

"Monstrous…a murderer at large, and you can't catch him? I've never heard anything like it! Besides, that business in Paris—it was an accident. The poor, silly dear mistook the window for her sitting-room door—"

"I know all about that, Mr. Guild," said Bliss quietly. "I'd rather we didn't discuss that aspect of the matter. The only thing I can tell you is that, if I know The Ringer—and nobody has better reason for knowing him and his methods—he will try to keep his word. It's up to us to protect you. You're to employ no new servants without consulting me. I want a daily notification telling me where you're going and how you're spending your time. The Ringer is the only criminal in the world, so far as I know, who depends entirely upon his power of disguise. We haven't a photograph of him as himself at Scotland Yard, and I'm one of the few people who have seen him as himself."

Miska jibbed at the prospect of accounting for his movements in advance. He was, he said, a creature of impulse, and was never quite sure where he would be next. Besides which, he was going to Berlin—

"If you leave the country I will not be responsible for your life," said Bliss shortly, and the young man turned pale.

* * * *

At first he treated the matter as a joke, but as the weeks became a month the sight of the detective sitting by the side of his chauffeur, the unexpected appearance of a Scotland Yard man at his elbow wherever he moved, began to get on his nerves.

And then one night Bliss came to him with the devastating news.

"The Ringer is in England," he said.

Miska's face was ghastly.

"How—how do you know?" he stammered.

But Bliss was not prepared to explain the peculiar qualities of Wally the Nose, or the peculiar behaviour of the man with the red beard.

When Wally the Nose passed through certain streets in Notting Dale he chose daylight for the adventure, and he preferred that a policeman should be in sight. Not that any of the less law-abiding folk of Notting Dale had any personal reason for desiring Wally the least harm, for, as he protested in his pathetic, lisping way, "he never did no harm" to anybody in Notting Dale.

He lived in a back room in Clewson Street, a tiny house rented by a deaf old woman who had had lodgers even more unsavoury than Wally, with his greasy, threadbare clothes, his big, protruding teeth, and his silly, moist face.

He came one night furtively to Inspector Stourbridge at the local police station, having been sent for.

"There's goin' to be a bust' at Lowes, the jewellers, in Islington, tomorrer, Mr. Stourbridge; some lads from Nottin' Dale are in it, and Elfus is fencin' the stuff. Is that what you wanted me about?"

He stood, turning his hat in his hands, his ragged coat almost touching the floor, his red eyelids blinking. Stourbridge had known many police informers, but none like Wally.

He hesitated, and then, with a "Wait here," he went into a room that led from the charge room and closed the door behind him.

Chief Inspector Bliss sat at a table, his head on his hand, turning over a thick dossier of documents that lay on the table before him.

"That man I spoke to you about is here, sir—the nose. He's the best we've ever had, and so long as he hasn't got to take any extraordinary risk —or doesn't know he's taking it—he'll be invaluable."

Bliss pulled at his little beard and scowled.

"Does he know why you have brought him here now?" he asked.

Stourbridge grinned.

"No—I put him on to inquire about a jewel burglary—but we knew all about it beforehand."

"Bring him in."

Wally came shuffling into the private room, blinked from one to the other with an ingratiating grin.

"Yes, sir?" His voice was shrill and nervous.

"This is Mr. Bliss, of Scotland Yard," said Stourbridge, and Wally bobbed his head.

"Heard about you, sir," he said, in his high, piping voice. "You're the bloke that got The Ringer—"

"To be exact, I didn't," said Bliss gruffly, "but you may."

"Me, sir?" Wally's mouth was open wide, his protruding rabbit's teeth suggested to Stourbridge the favourite figure of a popular comic artist. "I don't touch no Ringer, sir, with kind regards to you. If there's any kind of work you want me to do, sir, I'll do it. It's a regular 'obby of mine—I ought to have been in the p'lice. Up in Manchester they'll tell you all about me. I'm the feller that found Spicy Brown when all the Manchester busies was lookin' for him."

"That's why Manchester got a bit too hot for you, eh, Wally?" said Stourbridge.

The man shifted uncomfortably.

"Yes, they was a bit hard on me—the lads, I mean. That's why I come back to London. But I can't help nosing, sir, and that's a fact."

"You can do a little nosing for me," interrupted Bliss.

And thereafter a new and a more brilliant spy watched the movements of the man with the red beard.

* * * *

He had arrived in London by a ship which came from India but touched at Marseilles. He had on his passport the name of Tennett. He had travelled third-class. He was by profession an electrical engineer. Yet, despite his seeming poverty, he had taken a small and rather luxurious flat in Kensington.

It was his presence in Carlton House Terrace one evening that had first attracted the attention of Mr. Bliss. He came to see Guild, he said, on the matter of a project connected with Indian water power. The next day he was seen prospecting the house from the park side.

Ordinarily, it would have been a very simple matter to have pulled him in and investigated his credentials; but quite recently there had been what the Press had called a succession of police scandals. Two perfectly innocent men had been arrested in mistake for somebody else, and Scotland Yard was chary of taking any further risks.

Tennett was traced to his flat, and he was apparently a most elusive man, with a habit of taking taxicabs in crowded thoroughfares. What Scotland Yard might not do officially, it could do, and did do, unofficially. Wally the Nose listened with apparent growing discomfort.

"If it's him, he's mustard," he said huskily. "I don't like messing about with no Ringers. Besides, *he* hasn't got a red beard."

"Oh, shut up!" snarled Bliss. "He could grow one, couldn't he? See what you can find out about him. If you happen to get into his flat and see any papers lying about, they might help you. I'm not suggesting you should do so, but if you did…"

Wally nodded wisely.

In three days he furnished a curious report to the detective who was detailed to meet him. The man with the red beard had paid a visit to Croydon aerodrome and had made inquiries about a single-seater taxi to carry him to the Continent. He had spent a lot of his time at an electrical supply company in the East End of London, and had made a number of mysterious purchases which he had carried home with him in a taxicab.

Bliss consulted his superior.

"Pull him in," he suggested. "You can get a warrant to search his flat."

9

"His flat's been searched. There's nothing there of the slightest importance," reported Bliss.

He called that night at Carlton House Terrace and found Mr. Miska Guild a very changed man. These three months had reduced him to a nervous wreck.

"No news?" he asked apprehensively when the detective came in. "Has that wretched little creature discovered anything? By gad! he's as clever as any of you fellows. I was talking with him last night. He was outside on the Terrace with one of your men. Now, Bliss, I'd better tell you the truth about this girl in Paris—"

"I'd rather you didn't," said Bliss, almost sternly.

He wanted to preserve, at any rate, a simulation of interest in Mr. Guild's fate.

* * * *

He had hardly left Carlton House Terrace when a taxicab drove in and Wally the Nose almost fell into the arms of the detective.

"Where's Bliss?" he squeaked. "That red-whiskered feller's disappeared... left his house, and he's shaved off his beard, Mr. Connor. I didn't recognise him when he come out. When I made inquiries I found he'd gorn for good."

"The chief's just gone," said Connor, worried.

He went into the vestibule and was taken up to the floor on which Mr. Guild had his suite. The butler led him to the dining-room, where there was a phone connection, and left Wally the Nose in the hall. He was standing there disconsolately when Mr. Guild came out.

"Hullo! What's the news?" he asked quickly.

Wally the Nose looked left and right.

"He's telephonin' to the boss," he whispered hoarsely, "but I ain't told him about the letter."

He followed Miska into the library and gave that young man a piece of news that Mr. Guild never repeated.

He was waiting in the hall below when Connor came down.

"It's all right—they arrested old red whiskers at Liverpool Street Station. We had a man watching him as well."

Wally the Nose was pardonably annoyed.

"What's the use of having me and then puttin' a busy on to trail him?" he demanded truculently. "That's what I call double-crossing."

"You hop off to Scotland Yard and see the chief," said Connor, and Wally, grumbling audibly, vanished in the darkness.

The once red-bearded man sat in Inspector Bliss's private room, and he was both indignant and frightened.

"I don't know that there's any law preventing me taking off my beard, is there?" he demanded. "I was just going off to Holland, where I'm seeing a man who's putting money into my power scheme."

Bliss interrupted with a gesture.

"When you came to England you were broke, Mr. Tennett, and yet immediately you reached London you took a very expensive flat, bought yourself a lot of new clothes, and seemingly have plenty of money to travel on the Continent. Will you explain that?"

The man hesitated.

"Well, I'll tell you the truth. When I got to London I was broke, but I got into conversation with a fellow at the station who told me he was interested in engineering. I explained my power scheme to him, and he was interested. He was not the kind of man I should have thought would have had any money, yet he weighed in with two hundred pounds, and told me just what I had to do. It was his idea that I should take the flat. He told me where to go every day and what to do. I didn't want to part with the old beard, but he made me do that in the end, and then gave me three hundred pounds to go to Holland."

Bliss looked at him incredulously.

"Did he also suggest you should call at Carlton House Terrace and interview Mr. Guild?"

Tennett nodded.

"Yes, he did. I tell you, it made me feel that things weren't right. I wasn't quite sure of him, mind you, Mr. Bliss; he was such a miserable-looking devil—a fellow with rabbit's teeth and red eyelids...."

* * * *

Bliss came to his feet with a bound, stared across at Stourbridge, who was in the room.

"Wally!" he said.

A taxicab took him to Carlton House Terrace. Connor told him briefly what had happened.

"Did Wally see Mr. Guild?"

"Not that I know," said Connor, shaking his head.

Bliss did not wait for the lift; he flew up the stairs, met the footman in the hall.

"Where's Mr. Guild?"

"In his room, sir."

"Have you seen him lately?"

The man shook his head.

"No, sir; I never go unless he rings for me. He hasn't rung for half an hour."

11

Bliss turned the handle of the door and walked in. Miska Guild was lying on the hearthrug in the attitude of a man asleep, and when he turned him over on his back and saw his face Bliss knew that the true story of the chorus-girl and her "suicide" would never be told.

Chapter 2

Case Of The Home Secretary

There were two schools of thought at Scotland Yard. There were those who believed that The Ringer worked single-handed, and those who were convinced that he controlled an organisation and had the assistance of at least half a dozen people.

Inspector Bliss was of the first school, and instanced the killing of Miska Guild in proof.

"He's entirely on his own," he said. "Even his helper in that case was an innocent man who had no idea he was being used to attract the attention of the police."

"By the way, is there any news of him?" asked the Assistant Commissioner.

Bliss shook his head.

"He's in London; I was confident of that—now I know. If you had told me, sir, a few years ago, that any man could escape the police by disguise I should have laughed. But this man's disguises are perfect. He *is* the character he pretends to be. Take Wally the Nose, with his rabbit's teeth and his red eyes. Who would have imagined that a set of fake teeth worn over his others and a little colouring to his eyelids, plus the want of a shave, would be sufficient to hide him from me? I am one of the few people who have seen him without make-up, and yet he fooled me."

"Why do you think he is in London?"

Chief Inspector Bliss took out his pocket-case and, opening this, searched the papers it contained for a letter.

"It came this morning."

Colonel Walford stared up at him.

"From The Ringer?"

Bliss nodded.

"Typewritten on the same machine he used when he wrote to Miska Guild—the 's' is out of alignment and the tails of the 'p's' are worn."

Colonel Walford put on his glasses and read:

"Michael Benner, now under sentence of death, is innocent. I think you knew this when you gave evidence against him at the Old Bailey, for you

13

brought out every point in his favour. Lee Lavinski killed the old man, but was disturbed by Benner before he could get the loot. Lee left for Canada two days after the murder. Be a good fellow and help save this man."

There was no signature.

"What's the idea?" The Commissioner looked up over his glasses.

"The Ringer is right," said Bliss quietly. "Benner did not kill old Estholl —and I have discovered that Lavinski was in England when the murder was committed."

The crime of which he spoke was one of those commonplace crimes which excite little interest, since the guilt of the man accused seemed beyond doubt and the issue of the trial a foregone conclusion. Estholl was a rich man of seventy, who lived in a small Bloomsbury hotel. He was in the habit of carrying around large sums of money—a peculiar failing of all men who have risen from poverty to riches by their own efforts.

At four o'clock one wintry morning a guest at the hotel, who had been playing cards in his sitting-room with a party of friends, came out into the corridor and saw Benner, who was the night porter, emerge from the old man's room, carrying in his hand a bloodstained hammer. The man's face was white, he seemed dazed, and when challenged was speechless.

Rushing into the room the guest saw old Estholl lying on the bed in a pool of blood, dead. The porter's story after his arrest was that he had heard the old man's bell ring and had gone up to his room and knocked. Having no answer he opened the door and went in. He saw the hammer lying on the bed and picked it up mechanically, being so horrified that he did not know what he was doing.

* * * *

Benner was a young married man and in financial difficulties. He was desperately in need of money and had tried that evening to borrow seven pounds from the manageress of the hotel. Moreover, he had said to the head porter, "Look at old Estholl! If I had half of the money that he has in his pocket I shouldn't be worrying my head off tonight!"

Protesting his innocence, Benner went to the Old Bailey, and, after a trial which lasted less than a day, was condemned.

"The hammer was the property of the hotel, and Benner had access to the workroom where it was usually kept," said Bliss; "but, as against that, the workroom, which is in the hotel basement, was the easiest to enter from the outside, and the window was, in fact, found open in the morning."

"Is there any hope for Benner?"

Bliss shook his head.

"No. The Court has dismissed his appeal—and Strathpenner is not the kind of man who would have mercy; old Estholl was, unfortunately, a friend of his."

The Commissioner looked at the letter again, and ran his fingers through his hair irritably.

"Why should The Ringer bother his head about Benner?" he asked, and the ghost of a smile appeared on the bearded face of the detective.

"The trouble with the Ringer is that he can't mind his own business," he said. "That little note means that he is in the case—he doesn't drop letters around unless he's vitally interested; and if he's vitally interested in Benner, then we're going to see something rather dramatic. By the way, the Home Secretary has sent for me in connection with this affair."

"Is he likely to be influenced by you, inspector?" asked Colonel Walford drily.

"If I agree with him, yes; if I don't, no," said Bliss.

He went back to his room to learn that a visitor had called, and before his secretary told him her name he guessed her identity.

She was a pretty girl, despite the haggard lines which told of sleepless nights. She was dressed much better than when he had seen her at the Old Bailey.

"Well, Mrs. Benner," he said kindly, "what can I do?"

Her lips quivered.

"I don't know, sir.... I know Jim is innocent. He's incapable of doing such a horrible thing. I called at the Home Office, but the gentleman wouldn't see me."

Again Bliss looked at her clothes: they were obviously new. As though she read his thoughts: "I'm not in a bad way, sir—for money, I mean. A gentleman sent me twenty five-pound notes last week, and that paid off all poor Jim's debts and left me enough to live on for a bit."

"Who sent the money?" asked Bliss quickly, but here she could not give him information. It had arrived by post and was unaccompanied by any card or name.

"It might have been a woman who sent it?" suggested Bliss, though he knew better. "There was no letter at all?"

She shook her head.

"Only a piece of paper. I've got it here."

She fumbled in her bag and produced a strip of paper torn off the edge of a newspaper, on which was typed "DON'T LOSE HOPE."

* * * *

The "s" was out of alignment, the tail of the "p" was faint. Bliss smiled to himself, but it was a grim smile.

"You're under distinguished patronage," he said ironically, and then, in a more serious tone: "I'm afraid I can do very little for you. I am seeing—one of the officials at the Home Office this morning, but I'm afraid, Mrs. Benner, you'll have to resign yourself to—"

He did not finish his sentence, as he saw her eyes close and her face grow a shade paler.

Bliss pulled out a chair and bade her sit down; and somehow the sight of this woman in her agony brought a pang to a heart not easily touched.

"No hope?" she whispered, and shook her head in anticipation of his answer.

"A very faint one, I'm afraid," said the detective.

"But you don't think he's guilty, Mr. Bliss? When I saw Jim in Pentonville he told me that you didn't think so. It is horrible, horrible! He couldn't have done such an awful thing!"

Bliss was thinking rapidly. He had a dim idea of The Ringer's methods, and now he was searching here and there to find the avenue by which this ruthless man might approach the case.

"Have you any relations?"

She shook her head.

"No brothers?"

Again she gave him the negative.

"Good! Now, Mrs. Benner, I'll do the best I can for you, and in return I want you to do something for me. If the man who sent you that money approaches you, or if anybody who is unknown to you calls on you or asks you to meet them, I want you to telephone me here."

He scribbled down the number on a slip of paper and passed it across to her. "If anybody comes to you purporting to be from Scotland Yard, or to have any position of authority whatever, I want you to telephone to me about that also. I'm going to do what I can for your husband, and, though I'm afraid it isn't much, it will be my best."

It was half-past two when he arrived at the Home Office, and, by some miracle, Mr. Strathpenner had arrived. He was the despair of his subordinates, a man without method or system. There were days when he would not come to the office at all; other and more frequent days when he would put in an appearance an hour before the staff left, with the result that they were kept working into the night.

The Right Honourable William Strathpenner, His Majesty's principal Secretary of State, was a singularly unpopular man, both in and outside his party. He was pompous, unimaginative, a little uncouth of speech, intolerable. He had worn his way into the Cabinet as other men had done before him; not by genius of oratory or by political character, but the sheer weight of him had rubbed a place through which he had fallen, first to a minor office under the Crown, and then, by a succession of lucky accidents, to the highest of the subordinate Cabinet positions.

A thin man, short-necked, broad-shouldered, he had the expression of one who was constantly smelling something unpleasant. Political cartoonists had helped to make his face familiar, for his was an easy subject for caricature. The heavy, black, bristling eyebrows, the thick-lens spectacles, the bald head with the black wisps brushed across, his reddish nose—a libel on him, since he was a lifelong abstainer—made him unpleasant to look upon. He was almost as unpleasant to hear, for he had a harsh, grating voice and punctuated his sentences with an irritating little cough.

He kept Bliss waiting twenty minutes before he was admitted to the august presence; and there seemed no reason for the delay, for Mr. Strathpenner was reading a newspaper when he came in. He looked at the slip which announced the name of his visitor.

"Bliss, Bliss? Of course. Yes, yes, you're a police officer—ahem! This Benner case...yes, I remember now; I asked you to see me—ahem!"

He blinked across the table at Bliss, and his face had more than ever that unpleasant-smell expression.

"Now what do you know about this, hey? I haven't seen the Judge, but there's no doubt in my mind that this blackguard should suffer the extreme penalty of the law. This report, of course, is bunkum." He tapped the newspaper with his finger. "The usual bunkum—ahem! I don't believe in confessions—you don't believe in confessions?"

"Confessions, sir?" The inspector gazed at him in astonishment.

"Haven't you seen it?" Strathpenner threw the paper across the table. "There it is. Use your eyes...third column...."

* * * *

It was not in the third, but the fifth column, and the item of news was headed: "Hotel Murder Confession. Remarkable Statement by Red-handed Murderer."

Ottawa.

A man named Lavinski, who shot two policemen in cold blood in the streets of Montreal last night, when detected in the act of breaking into the Canadian Bank, and was shot by a third policeman, has made a remarkable statement before a magistrate who was called to his bedside at the hospital.

Lavinski is not expected to recover from his wounds, and in the course of his statement he said that he was responsible for the murder of Mr. Estholl, for which a man named Benner lies under sentence of death in London. Lavinski says that he made an entrance to the hotel knowing that Mr. Estholl carried large sums of money in his pocket, that he took a hammer intending to use the claw to open the door in case it was locked.

17

Estholl woke up as he entered the room, and Lavinski says that he struck him with the hammer, though he was not aware that he had inflicted a fatal injury. He then discovered that the dead man had a hanging bell-push in his hand, and fearing that he had rung it, he made his escape without attempting to search his pockets. The statement has been attested before a magistrate.

Bliss looked up and met the Home Secretary's gaze.

"Well? Bunkum, eh? You've had no official notification at Scotland Yard?"

"No, sir."

"I thought not; I thought not—ahem! An old trick, eh, inspector? You've had that sort of thing played on you before. It won't save Benner, I assure you—ahem! I assure you!"

Bliss gaped at him.

"But you're not going to hang this man until you get this statement over from Canada?"

"Don't be absurd, inspector, don't be absurd! If a Secretary of State were to be influenced by newspaper reports where would he be, eh? Did you read the last paragraph?"

Bliss took up the paper again and saw, later:

The man Lavinski died before he could sign the statement he had made before Mr. Prideaux.

"Let me tell you, sir"—Mr. Strathpenner wagged an admonitory finger—"His Majesty's Secretary of State is not to be influenced by wild-cat stories of this kind...by newspaper reports, by—ahem!—hearsay evidence as it were. What are we to do? I ask you! On the unsigned deposition of a—er—convicted murderer caught in the act. Release this man Benner?"

"You could grant him a respite, sir," interrupted Bliss.

Mr. Strathpenner sat back in his chair and his tone became icy.

"I am not asking your advice, inspector.... If I lose my pocket-book or my watch I have no doubt your advice will be invaluable—ahem! to secure its recovery. Thank you, inspector."

He waved Bliss from the room. The detective went across to Scotland Yard, but Walford had gone. The only thing he knew was that the death warrant had not been signed. It is part of the Home Secretary's duty to affix his name to a document that will send a fellow-creature from this life, and one of the bravest men who ever sat in a Cabinet refused the second offer of the office for this reason.

Mr. Strathpenner, at any rate, was not in any way distressed by his duty. He had summoned the Judge who had tried the case to meet him the next day, and he went back to his house in Crowborough that night without a single qualm or misgiving.

* * * *

He was a widower; lived alone except for a large staff of servants, which included a French *chef*, and he dined, a solitary figure in the big mahogany-panelled dining-room, a large German philosophical work propped up before him, for he was an excellent linguist and had a weakness for shallow philosophies if they were propounded with sufficient pretentiousness.

He was so reading at the end of his meal when the visitor was announced. Mr. Strathpenner looked at the card suspiciously. It read: "Mr. James Hagger, 14, High Street, Crouchstead."

Now, Crouchstead was the West of England constituency which had the honour of being represented in Parliament by the Home Secretary, and, since he held his seat by the narrowest of majorities, he resisted the temptation to send the message which rose too readily to his lips.

"All right, show him in here."

He looked at the card again. Who was Mr. Hagger? Probably somebody very important in Crouchstead; somebody he had shaken hands with, probably. An important member of the Crouchstead Freedom Club, likely enough. Mr. Strathpenner loathed Crouchstead and all its social manifestations; yet he screwed a smile into his face when Mr. Hagger was ushered to his presence.

The visitor proved to be a very respectably dressed man, with a heavy black moustache which drooped beneath chin level.

"You remember me, sir?" His voice was deep and solemn. "I met you at the Freedom banquet. I'm the secretary of the Young Workers' League."

Oh, it was the Young Workers' League, was it? thought Mr. Strathpenner. He had almost forgotten its existence.

"Of course…naturally…sit down, Mr. Hagger. Will you have a glass of port?"

Mr. Hagger deposited his hat carefully on the floor.

"No, sir, thank you, I'm a lifelong abstainer. I neither touch, taste, nor handle. Of course, I realise that a gentleman like you has to have likker in the 'ouse. It's about this man Benner…."

The Minister stiffened.

"We've been 'aving a talk, some of the leaders of the party in Crouchstead, and we've come to the conclusion it'd be a great mistake to hang that man—"

Mr. Strathpenner shook his head sadly.

"Ah, Mr. Hagger, you've no idea how deeply I have considered this subject, and with what reluctance I have been compelled, or shall be compelled, to allow the law to take its course. You realise that a man in my position…."

He continued his justification in terms which he had applied before to stray members of Parliament who had strolled into his room in the House of Commons, and had expressed views similar to those which Mr. Hagger was on the point of enunciating.

"Now, let us leave this—er—unpleasant subject. Will you take some coffee with me? By the way, how did you come?"

"I was brought up from the station in a fly," said Mr. Hagger.

He was very apologetic.

"You quite understand, Mr. Strathpenner, that I had to do my duty. The committee paid my fare up, and I thought it'd be a good chance of seeing you. I've heard about your wonderful house, and I didn't want to miss the chance of seeing it."

Here he touched the Home Secretary on his soft side. The house had an historic as well as an artistic value; it was one of the innumerable John o' Gaunt hunting lodges that stud the county of Sussex. It was indubitably pre-Elizabethan. Mr. Strathpenner was prouder of his home than of any of his attainments. He led the visitor from room to room and was almost genial in his response to the visitor's interest.

"...Haunted, of course—all these old places are haunted. There's a dungeon...the previous owner used it as a coal-cellar! A Philistine, sir—a boor —ahem!—or something objectionable. Come this way."

He opened a stout oak door and preceded his visitor down a flight of stone stairs; showed him not only the dungeon, which had been carefully restored to its earlier grimness, but a lower prison chamber, six feet by six, approached through a stone trapdoor.

"Let me show you...."

He went before the other down the ladder.

"We have ringbolts here, almost worn through with age, where the unfortunate prisoners were chained. And yet the place is fairly well ventilated."

"It's a funny thing," said Mr. Hagger, as he carefully descended the ladder, "that the flyman who brought me up from the station told me to be sure to ask you to show me your dungeon."

"Extraordinary," said Mr. Strathpenner, not ill-pleased. "But the place has quite a local reputation."

* * * *

His Majesty's judges are not to be kept waiting. Sir Charles Jean, the senior Common Law Judge, looked at his watch and closed the case with a vicious snap.

"The Home Secretary said that he would be here at half-past four."

20

"I'm very sorry, sir," said the official who was with him. "I've been on the phone to Mr. Strathpenner. He left the house an hour ago and should be here at any moment. It's rather foggy, and he is a very nervous traveller."

"Where is his secretary, Mr. Cliney?"

"He has gone down to Crowborough with some documents for signature —he had only gone ten minutes when Mr. Strathpenner phoned through."

"I'm afraid I can wait no longer. I will see him in the morning. I hope you'll impress upon Mr. Strathpenner that there is, in my mind, a very grave doubt about Benner's guilt."

He might have added that he did not think that would have very much influence with the Minister, who had on a previous occasion ignored the recommendation of a judge.

He had hardly gone before the official heard the rasping voice and nervous cough of his chief, and hurried into the secretary's office.

"Sir Charles Jean, eh? And gone? Ahem! Well, well, well! I can't be at the beck and call of judges, my dear man. Or Ringers either, my friend, eh? —ahem!—or Ringers either!"

"Ringers, sir?" said the astonished official.

There was a dry, rasping chuckle.

"Visited me last night, the scoundrel—ahem! That will be something to tell Mr. What's-his-name-Bliss. By the way, call him up and tell him that when I return from Paris on Friday I should like to see him."

"Paris, sir?" asked the startled official. "There is a meeting of the Cabinet on Friday morning."

"I know, I know," testily.

He opened a portfolio, took out a sheet of paper and stared at it owlishly. The official saw the document and thought it a moment to pass along the message.

"Sir Charles asked me to tell you that he is very doubtful as to whether this man should be executed—"

But the other was scrawling his name.

"There will be a respite of fourteen days," he said. "The matter may come up for consideration next Wednesday after the arrival of the depositions from Canada."

He blotted the sheet and pushed it across to the Under-Secretary.

"The respite may be announced in the newspapers," he said.

* * * *

"I ought to have known," said Bliss ruefully, "that Strathpenner was the easiest man in the world to impersonate. The curious thing is, it did strike me when I was talking to him."

"How is he?" asked Walford.

21

"When they released him from his lower dungeon," said Bliss, with the ghost of a smile in his eyes, "he was slightly insane, but not, I think, quite so insane as Mr. Hagger of Crouchstead, who is no longer a lifelong abstainer. Mr. Strathpenner used the lower dungeon as a wine cellar, and they had to live on something. They might be living there still if The Ringer hadn't been obliging enough to send me a wire."

22

Chapter 3

The Murderer Of Many Names

I

Mr. Ellroyd arrived in England six months after the Meister murder, when the police of the world were searching for one Henry Arthur Milton, "otherwise" (as the police bills stated in eighteen languages) "known as 'The Ringer.'"

They translated "The Ringer" variously and sometimes oddly, but, whether he saw it in Czecho-Slovakian or in the Arabic of Egypt, the reader knew that this Henry Arthur Milton was a man who could change his appearance with the greatest rapidity.

Perhaps not quite so readily as Mr. Ellroyd could and did change his name.

In Australia, which was his home, he was Li Baran; in Chicago he was Bud Fraser, Al Crewson, Jo Lemarque, Hop Stringer, and plain Jock. Under these pseudonyms he was wanted for murder in the first degree, for he was a notorious gunman and bank robber.

In New York he bore none of these names, but several others. Canada knew him as a bigamist who had married under three different names, one of which was the Hon. John Templar-Statherby.

He came to England from Malta (of all places in the world), and he came handicapped with a Ringer complex. Now the vanity of the criminal is a matter which has formed the subject of many monographs, and Joseph Ellroyd, in spite of his poise, his middle age, and his undoubted philosophy, was vain to a degree.

He wanted the publicity of The Ringer, and in his first unlawful act (which was the daylight hold-up of the Streatham Bank) he publicly identified himself with The Ringer.

If you think it extraordinary in a man whose one desire in life should have been to preserve a modest anonymity and pursue his own peculiar graft, attracting as little attention to himself as possible, you make no allowance for his complex, or, as Superintendent Bliss said, for his desire to put the police on the wrong track. Bliss was wrong. Joe's chief urge was vanity.

He derived immense satisfaction from the sensation which resulted. "Again The Ringer!" said a flaming headline. The phrase tickled Mr. Ellroyd. His second *coup* was a little less spectacular—the smashing of an hotel safe. But what it lacked in news value as a piece of craftsmanship (though the haul subsequently proved to be a large one) was compensated by the three words scrawled across the safe door: "AGAIN THE RINGER!"

A month later Mr. Joe Ellroyd went to his bedroom to change for dinner. He was staying at the Piccadilly Plaza Hotel, for he was a gentlemanly man and a classy dresser. He entered the room switching on the light and closing the door.

When he turned he looked first into the muzzle of a large Browning pistol and then into the completely masked face of the man who held it.

"Ellroyd your name is, isn't it?"

Joe blinked at the gun, and his hand dropped carelessly to his pocket.

"Keep 'em up!" said the stranger. "This gun doesn't make much noise, and I could catch you before you fell. My name is Henry Arthur Milton—I am wanted by the police for killing a gentleman who deserved to die."

"My God—'The Ringer'!" gasped Joe.

"The Ringer—exactly. You are using my name to cover certain vulgar robberies—you are wanted for other and worse offences in various parts of the world. I object to my name being used by a cheap skate of a gunman. I have a greater objection to its use by a thief. I have taken a lot of trouble to find you, and my original intention was to hand you over to the mortuary keeper. I am giving you a chance."

"Listen, Milton—" began Joe.

"I am warning you. I shall not warn you again. If you are a wise man you will not need a second warning. That is all. Step over here—and step quickly!"

Joe obeyed. The man moved to the door, and the lights went out.

"Don't move—you're against the window and I can see you."

A second later the door opened and closed. There was the sound of a snapping lock.

Joe, breathing heavily, went cautiously forward, turned on the lights and tried the door. It was, as he suspected, locked. But there was a telephone….

Before he picked up the instrument he saw the cut of trailing wires.

"The Ringer!" he breathed, and sat down heavily on his bed, wiping the cold perspiration from his face. It was remarkable that there was perspiration to wipe, for Joe was the coolest man that ever shot a policeman.

For two years after this he lived without offence, as he could well afford to do, for he was a comparatively rich man.

And then one day in Berlin....

* * * *

"Auf wiedersehen!"

The perfect stranger, with the elaborate friendliness which is too often the attribute of his kind, flourished his hat extravagantly.

"So long!" said Henry Arthur Milton, coldly indifferent.

Why this sudden activity? he wondered. He passed out on to the Friedrichstrasse and nobody would imagine that he was in the slightest degree concerned with the big fat man he had left at the entrance to the *bahnhof*. His fingers said "snap!" to a watchful taxi-driver.

"Kutscher! Do you see that gentleman in the black coat with the fur collar?"

"Most certainly: the Jew!"

Arthur Milton nodded approvingly and opened and closed the door of the taxi once or twice in an absent-minded manner.

"Is that insight or eyesight?" he asked.

"I know him," said the *kutscher* complacently. "He is from Frankfort and his name is Sahl—a dealer in sausages."

Mr. Milton inclined his head.

"A local industry," he said lightly. "Now, my friend, drive me to the Hôtel Zweinerman und Spiez."

It was a very comfortable taxi: Berlin is famous for the luxury of these public vehicles, but it *was* a taxi. There was nothing remarkable about it except that its driver had ignored the summons of half a dozen of the passengers who had arrived by the Hamburg express, and had instantly responded to the signal of Henry Arthur Milton. But there was no spring lock on the door—he had tried that before he got in. And the driver was following the conventional route.

Mr. Milton stroked his dark toothbrush moustache. His colouring gave him a somewhat saturnine appearance. His black glossy hair, his heavy black eyebrows, a marked lugubriousness of expression, corrected the attractions of good features and rather nice eyes.

Before the barrack façade of the hotel the cab stopped. Milton gripped his suitcase and alighted.

"Wait for me, I shall be five minutes."

The hotel porter stood at the open door of the cab, his face set in the hospitable smile for which he was engaged. He sought to secure the suitcase, but was frustrated.

"Is Mr. Pffiefer in the hotel?"

The porter would see—immediately. Arthur Milton followed him into the hotel; but when the porter, having inquired, discovered that Mr.

Pffiefer's name did not appear in the guest list, and turned to inform the elegant Englishman, he had vanished. There was an elevator opening from the vestibule, and into this Arthur Milton had stepped.

Truthfully speaking, quite a number of so-called coincidences are interpretable into inevitable effects of quite logical causes. The Hôtel Zweinerman, for example: one gravitated there naturally. Englishmen were swept into the Zweinerman as by some mystic force.

As to the second floor—Mr. Milton chose the second floor because thereon were large and often unoccupied suites. He knew the hotel this way and that way, as the saying goes, and he knew that the largest, the most expensive suite usually reserved for plutocrats in a hurry was that which was to the right front of the elevator. So that, if there had been any English plutocrat rushing through the capital in mad haste, No. 9 would be his suite.

He tried the door of No. 9, opened it boldly, as a man might who had made a genuine mistake. It was a large bedroom, floridly decorated, furnished heavily. The room was empty; obviously it had not been occupied for some days—obviously, at any rate, to Henry Arthur Milton, who had the gift of observation.

There was a small calendar on the mantelpiece, an oxidised silver frame with a day in large letters. The day was "Mittwoch," 7th, which was Wednesday—it was now Friday, the 9th, but the chambermaid had not turned the little knob which would bring the calendar up to date.

Between the bed and the bathroom door was a writing-table—an unusual position, for the writer would sit in his or her own light. And on the table was a pale pink blotting-pad, which Milton would not have favoured with a second glance—only the writing was in English.

He reconnoitred the bathroom before he made any other inspection of the pad. From the bathroom a second door gave access to a sitting-room. Escape was a simple matter.

Detaching the top sheet of blotting-paper, he carried it to the bathroom and bolted the door. There was no mistaking the "B" or the firm, masculine "M"—they were not in German or Latin handwriting.

Milton read slowly.

"Suffering snakes!" he breathed.

It was the name of the man to whom the letter was addressed which excited his profanity. The significance of the florid preamble did not come home to him until he read, later, the London telegram in the *Deutsche Allgemeine Zeitung*.

"Bless my soul!" said Mr. Milton, and, going into the bathroom, locked the door. A hot, wet towel wiped his eyebrows from existence (they had taken him an hour to fix before he left Hamburg); the toothbrush moustache yielded instantly to the same treatment. Opening his suitcase, he took out a light fawn coat and a shapeless hat....

* * * *

There went down the lift a man with a somewhat vacuous expression. He wore large rimless glasses and a vivid necktie. His face was hairless, his head so closely cropped that it might have been shaved. In the vestibule he saw the big sausage-maker from Frankfort interviewing the manager. With him was another detective.

Milton shuffled up to the reception clerk, grief in his voice and tone.

"I have brought for the gentleman of No. 9 an account. But he is gone."

"Account!"

A reception clerk dealing with nobodies is altogether a different person from a reception clerk dealing with somebodies.

"You should have brought it when the gentleman was here," he grumbled. Nevertheless he turned the pages of a book. "Mr. Smith, 249, Doughty Street," he said in English.

"Do not give addresses!"

His companion was obviously in authority. The book closed with a bang.

"Write!" he barked.

Mr. Milton shuffled forth humbly.

The cab-driver who had brought him to the Zweinerman stood guard in the doorway.

"I want a cab—" began the hairless man, peering short-sightedly through his glasses.

"Engaged!"

The new Mr. Milton passed into the street. Near the Tiergarten he bought the Government newspaper, and then he understood what all the bother was about:

THE RINGER IN BERLIN!

The So-Infamous English Criminal Traced to Germany....

("Good Lord!" said Henry Arthur Milton, and read on):

"Henry Arthur Milton, an English criminal, is believed to be in hiding in Berlin. Following an atrocious robbery and murder near London, the miscreant escaped to Germany, and has had the audacity to address a letter to Chief-Central Superintendent of Police Bliss...."

("They never get our titles right," he murmured)—

"...deriding the police efforts to capture him. That letter was posted in Berlin! The Ringer, as he is called, is a master of the art of

27

disguise and owes his name (Ringer of Changes) to that fact. The crime for which he is now sought by the Berlin police is…."

(The Ringer read on and on, a set grin on his face):

"…Hitherto The Ringer has killed, but has never robbed. Man after man he has slain for some wrong done either to himself or to humanity. But robbery has never before been his object…."

"Dear me!" said Henry Arthur Milton, still smiling mirthlessly. "That is certainly amusing! Joe has forgotten something!"

He left Berlin by the night train on a passport which described him as Eric Ressermanns, a native of Munchen. He went on board the English boat as Joseph Sampson, of Leeds. But that was not the name that he wrote in the guest book at the Craven Street Hotel.

He spent the whole of the next day examining the files of a newspaper for particulars of the interesting crime with which his name had been associated.

II

It was half-past two o'clock on a wet, cold morning when the mail van from London came out of the Great West Road and turned towards Colnbrook and Slough. A motor scout on duty at the juncture of the roads saw from his shelter the red-painted motor-van pass. It skidded as it turned (he afterwards stated), and he thought he heard the driver laugh.

The mail van was late, but, once out of the West Road, speeding would be impossible until Slough was passed. The road winds and turns abruptly and is rather narrow. Moreover, ahead of the driver was the narrower street of Colnbrook.

The van had travelled to within a mile of that village when the driver saw a red lamp in the road and jammed on his brakes. Ahead of him, in the light of his headlamps, he saw a man in shining oilskins, who was pointing to the side of the road.

He stopped the car, and, as he did so, the solitary wayfarer came out of the glare of the lamps into the patch of darkness level with the driver's seat.

"What is the matter?" It was the guard inside the van.

"Get down!"

The driver saw the automatic in the stranger's hand—saw it was pointed at him, and gripped the lever….

It was the sound of the shot which brought the guard leaping to the road, revolver in hand. He was alive when the police found him two hours later. The van had been driven into a field near the end of the Colnbrook by-pass.

28

He told his fragment of tale, but was dead before the magistrate arrived to take his statement.

There were two clues, so attenuated that Superintendent Bliss rejected the one and was baffled by the other.

A motor-cycle with sidecar had passed through Colnbrook at five minutes after three. It had been driven by a man in a brown leather coat who was talking to somebody in the sidecar—evidently a woman—for he addressed her as "my dear girl." To the police officer who saw him he shouted "Good-night." Ten minutes later he should have been in Slough, but was not seen in that town. There was, however, an explanation for this: he might have turned off on to the Windsor Road.

The second piece of evidence was on the mail van itself. Scrawled in chalk along the side were the words: "Again The Ringer!"

Mr. Bliss read this and his bearded lips curled derisively. He might sneer at this piece of bravado, but the country had for the moment lost its sense of humour. Newspaper columns protested at the "immunity of this arch-assassin." None the less, Mr. Bliss maintained his opinion.

* * * *

Colonel Walford, Assistant Commissioner of Police, leaned back in his padded chair, a wandering quill toothpick between his teeth, and listened.

"If it is The Ringer, then he has changed his method," said Superintendent Bliss. "You know, sir, that he has never killed except to fulfil some crazy vendetta of his—he's a man of means...why, you've told me the same thing a score of times!"

Colonel Walford shifted uneasily in his chair.

"Well...yes. But you can't get over the fact that the words 'Again The Ringer' were written in chalk on the mail van, that they were found scribbled on the safe door of the Rugeley Hotel—and you remember that Streatham Bank robbery.... Still...."

He was of two minds: Mr. Bliss had one.

"'Again The Ringer'!" he scoffed. "As if Milton would descend to that kind of tomfoolery! He has killed people—but there has been a reason behind it. He is a self-appointed executioner of nasty men."

The colonel shook his grey head.

"I don't know—this letter from Berlin in which he confesses he was the murderer...giving details which only he could know...." He shook his head again.

But Bliss was not convinced.

"One always gets these sham confessions—there was enough published the morning after the murder to supply a mischievous busy-body with all the information he required. The problem to me is: how did the murderer know that there was a registered package containing 160,000 American dollars in the van? I only found that out yesterday."

"Dollars? Why on earth?"

"The package was from the London Textile Bank to a Mr. Elliott, of Long Hall, near Slough. It was insured with underwriters, so that only the insurance people will be the losers."

"But why dollars?"

Bliss could supply an explanation. Mr. Elliott, a wealthy and a self-made man, dabbled in the fine arts. There was in the country at that moment the newly-discovered Maltby Velasquez. It was the property of a French dealer, who had stipulated, in view of the erratic behaviour of his native currency and an ingrained suspicion of sterling, that payment should be made in dollars.

"The picture has been bought to all intents and purposes, and was to have been delivered yesterday. I am seeing Mr. Elliott tonight."

"And if you see The Ringer—" began Walford.

"The Ringer? Huh!"

As he walked down the corridor a messenger handed him a telegram. Bliss read and nodded. On the whole, he was not sorry to get the intimation this telegram contained.

Mr. Forsythe Elliott, being a public-spirited man, might well have complained that none of the theories so ingeniously advanced by him in letter, even by telegram, had been accepted. Or, if the police had acted upon them, certainly there had been no acknowledgment of the inspiration.

He had seen Bliss for a few minutes.

"He treated the matter quite casually," he reported to his saturnine young secretary. "You might imagine that a double murder and robbery was an everyday occurrence! I have no wish to be hard on the police, but I do think...."

What Mr. Elliott did think he related at length.

And then, to his annoyance, coming back from a brisk country walk, his servant informed him that Mr. Bliss had not only arrived, but had been in the house for the greater part of an hour. Later he saw the bearded figure strolling aimlessly across the lawn, and wagged his finger in playful admonition, though in truth Mr. Elliott was very annoyed indeed.

"You said six," he said reproachfully. "Well, have you a clue? You look tremendously mysterious."

"I cannot afford to be mysterious," said the man from London quietly. "I have just been having a chat with your secretary."

"An extremely able young man," said Elliott.

"Young?" The bearded man shook his head. "He's not so young as he appears. Would you call him reliable?"

The eyebrows of Mr. Forsythe Elliott rose in amazement.

"Reliable? Well, I have had him for the greater part of six months."

"Then he must be reliable."

There was a touch of irony in the tone.

Mr. Elliott was all for dropping such unimportant matters as his secretary; was, indeed, ready to repeat and amplify the theories that he had already propounded.

"Obviously it is The Ringer," he said. "I have made a very careful study of this man. In fact, I have read every scrap of information I can beg, borrow, or buy."

"My view is," continued the undaunted master of Long Hall, "that he escaped from this country after the last affair, went to Germany—you, of course, know all about the letter, because it was addressed to you, according to the newspapers—and, being hard up—these fellows are invariably gamblers—he has returned and is living somewhere in this neighbourhood."

But his hearer gave him no encouragement. Not that Mr. Elliott required such a stimulus.

"My secretary says—and Leslie is something of a motor-cyclist—that this wretched assassin probably never uses the roads at all, but takes to the field paths."

"You surprise me," said his audience politely.

* * * *

In the few minutes he had alone with his secretary later Mr. Elliott expressed his utter lack of faith in the official police. The young man did not answer. Mr. Elliott thought he looked a little nervous. He had never known him so jumpy before. That night at dinner:

"You know The Ringer?"

"Very well indeed."

"He interests me tremendously" (Mr. Elliott was almost enthusiastic). "Although I cannot afford to lose so large a sum—as a matter of fact, I don't lose it at all, but if I did the fact that The Ringer was responsible gives the crime a certain cachet. Now, my theory…."

It was difficult even to contend against theories, for surely there was no atmosphere better calculated to put a man in good humour, even with the crankiest of cranks, than the raftered dining-room of Long Hall.

The cloth had been removed, the super-polished surface of the dark table reflected the long-stemmed port glasses. Mr. Elliott reached out and helped himself to another cigarette from the silver box and lit it with the glowing end of the first.

He was tall and broad-shouldered; good-looking in his rugged way. The untidy hair was streaked with grey; he looked all that he confessed himself to be—a man of the people who had come to fortune by his own industry. In every sense he was a contrast to the young man who sat on his left, gloomily absorbed in his own dark thoughts.

Leslie Carter's voice said "public school." His face was moulded more finely than his employer's, his hands were more shapely, his movements had something of an athletic grace. The sombre man sitting opposite, twisting the end of his little beard to a point, noticed that from time to time Mr. Elliott shot a puzzled glance at his secretary. And Leslie Carter's attitude throughout the meal had been a little puzzling. He had scarcely spoken a word, hardly raised his eyes from the plate, though his *vis-à-vis* had been the second prettiest girl Mr. Bliss had ever seen.

Sullen—sulking about something—worried? The visitor was not sure.

"…the third crime of the character committed during the past three months," Forsythe Elliott was saying; "and all occurring within a radius of twenty—say thirty—miles. That can only mean that our friend The Ringer has his headquarters in Berkshire."

"It was not The Ringer."

The other man shook his head emphatically, was about to say something else, but stopped himself. Instead, he looked swiftly from his host to the secretary, and Mr. Elliott understood. Presently:

"You might tell them to have the car ready for Mr. Bliss."

The young man looked up with a start.

"All right," he said, and rose.

When he had gone the visitor drew his chair nearer to where Elliott sat.

"What is his financial position?" asked Bliss.

Elliott shrugged his broad shoulders.

"He's always broke—that kind of kid always is."

"Have you asked him whether he told anybody about the money coming to you?"

His host shook his head.

"No; I have had no opportunity. He had to go to Germany—his brother, who is in Hamburg, sent for him."

"He went to Germany—when?"

Elliott considered.

"The day after the robbery. In any event, I should have let him go, but it happened that I went off to Paris to fix up about the picture. I should, in the ordinary course of events, have taken the money with me."

His guest tugged at his little beard.

"In Berlin, eh? The murder was committed on Monday night—he could have reached Berlin by Wednesday—the date the letter was posted—he could have been back here on Thursday. When did your secretary return?"

Mr. Elliott was obviously uncomfortable.

"Yesterday—Friday. But, good heavens! you don't suggest...?"

"I'm not suggesting anything," said the other. "I am merely following avenues of possibility. The fact is that I have already spoken to your secretary...do you mind if I talk to you outside? I have a strong objection to talking in a room."

Elliott went to the door.

"I hate wasting good wine, but I suppose you don't mind."

Elliott turned to see him looking admiringly at the ruby glass.

"Here's destruction to The Spurious Ringer!"

The host came back to the table and poured wine into his half-empty glass.

"That, Mr. Bliss, is a toast I can drink. At the same time, I'm not so sure that you're right."

He carried his argument into the night and past the waiting car. At the far end of the lawn were three high firs, and it was not until they reached these that Elliott stopped. He might not have stopped even then, but he stumbled over a coiled rope that lay on the grass.

"What the devil—" he checked himself and asked: "Now, what do you want to say about Leslie?"

"His brother was not ill—the telephone message which you passed on to him was a hoax. And a blundering hoax. Did you notice how worried he was at dinner?"

"I did notice," admitted Elliott, and the other laughed.

"He's worried because he found a small cottage on your estate that is supposedly empty, but which contains the motor-cycle and sidecar that the robber and murderer has been using. He put these two facts together—the fake phone message from London which took him to Germany in order that he might be incriminated, and the discovery of the cycle. Probably he has found out something else. I hadn't time to ask him."

"He told you this?"

"Yes, Joe, he told me this."

Joe Ellroyd (Forsythe Elliott was almost the toniest *alias* he had ever used) turned to fly, but a hand gripped his arm, and he felt curiously weak.

"You're doped, Joe—that last toast was my mercy! You went to Berlin and wrote a letter to Bliss. I found the blot of it—that was a coincidence. But I should have found you anyway. I think I warned you once before...."

* * * *

In the house a telephone bell rang, and the secretary answered it.

"Mr. Bliss? But Mr. Bliss is here, in the grounds with Elliott...!"

Bliss, at the other end of the wire, spoke quickly.

"I had a wire telling me not to come tonight. Phone the local police and have them up as quickly as you can...got a gun? Take it, arm the servants and search the grounds."

He himself arrived an hour later, but neither Elliott nor his visitor was found. It was not until the dawn came and showed the still figure swinging on a branch of the highest fir that Elliott's absence was explained.

When they got him down they found a half-sheet of paper, and a ten-pound note pinned to the dead man's sleeve.

Please give the bank-note to the public hangman and offer him my apologies for this invasion of his province.

There was no signature—but Inspector Bliss knew the writing.

Chapter 4

A Servant Of Women

Once upon a time, in those absurd days of war, when the laws governing the sanctity of human life were temporarily suspended, a flying officer, making a reconnaissance to the north-west of Bagdad, saw the solitary figure of a man lying in the desert land. By his side was a dead camel.

The flying officer, whose name was Henry Arthur Milton, dipped down to take a closer view, and as he did so he saw the man's hand raised feebly as though signalling for help.

Captain Milton shut off his engines, having found a likely landing-place, and five minutes later was examining the wounded man, a person of some importance, to judge by the trappings of his camel and his own raiment.

He was wounded in the shoulder, half delirious with thirst, and proved to be one Ibn el Masjik. He had been wounded in a skirmish with British troops, and after the rescuer had made him comfortable El Masjik had a request to make.

"I am the chief of a fighting clan and I could not survive the disgrace of being taken prisoner. Therefore I ask you as a favour that you take me to the city of my father, and I will give you my parole that I will not fight against your people, nor shall any of my tribe fight."

Milton spoke Arabic as though it were his mother-tongue. He was also a man of unconventional habits, and although he had no more authority to carry out the wishes of his prisoner than he had to take upon himself the command of the British Army in Mesopotamia, he did not hesitate.

His aeroplane made a journey of a hundred and seventy miles, landed within half a mile of the walled city of Khor, and at some risk to himself (for the local inhabitants were unaware of his errand of mercy) delivered the wounded man to the care of his friends.

"Come to me when this war is ended," said Ibn el Masjik; "and, though all the world be against you, I shall be for you. If you are poor, I will make you rich. My father's city is for your asking."

This time he spoke in English, for he had in his youth been educated at a preparatory school in Bournemouth, his father being a rich man with a leaning to Western ideals.

Henry Arthur Milton remembered this promise some years later, when he was hard pressed, and for six months was the guest of Ibn el Masjik, whose father was now dead. Mr. Milton saw the administration of an Eastern city and a Near Eastern people who snapped their scornful fingers at authority which was too far away to be effective.

This white-walled city stood on the edge of the wilderness, and time had passed it by. Raiding parties went out unashamed and returned laden with booty and slaves. Milton saw men and women sold in the market-place, saw life unchanged from what it had been in the days when Mahomet's uncle was guardian of the Kaaba, and the Prophet's disciples were praying in Medina.

One night Henry Arthur expostulated about certain practices, and the thin, ascetic face of Ibn el Masjik lit up in a smile. He tossed a half-smoked cigarette into a silver vase, lit another, and settled himself more comfortably on the cushions.

* * * *

They were in the dining-room of his palace—a tall, bare apartment, with lime-washed walls and vivid, silken colourings—and a Circassian girl sat at his feet and ate sweet-meats noisily.

"My friend," he said, "it is a far cry to Bournemouth, Hampshire. Slavery is merely a name for service, and it is a matter of form whether it takes the shape you see here in Khor, or in some dingy northern town where men and women have to leave their beds at the sound of a whistle and hurry through rain and sleet to the prison-houses you call factories. My slaves are more pleasantly treated: they have the sunshine; they are well fed; they sleep in their own houses."

He was perfectly frank about the traffic. There was a little port on the Red Sea where one could buy, under the very noses of a British administration, this kind of artisan—at a price.

"Not always can I buy what I desire," he explained. "My women ask me all the time for such a man, and where may he be found?" He sighed heavily. "Yes, the West is creeping upon us, and Kemal's new law concerning women has reached even here."

He shrugged his shoulders, smoothed his white silken robe more decorously about his knees, and smiled reminiscently.

"I do not object. There is a piquancy in the new custom which is very amusing. And we differ from most other tribes in that our women are never veiled, and have rights of choice."

After Milton came back to Western Europe he frequently corresponded with his blood brother, and at the back of his mind he always had Khor as a final sanctuary in case things went wrong.

The police might suspect that Henry Arthur Milton, whom they called The Ringer, had many homes, but they did not know where. There was, for example, a villa on the outskirts of Cannes, very convenient for a man who wished to make a rapid exit from one country to another. He rented a small flat overlooking the little *Sok* in Tangier; he had certainly a house which was a semi-detached residence at Norbury, and here he spent a greater part of his time than any of his enemies imagined.

There was a small garden at the back of the house which he cultivated, and across the dividing wall it often happened that he discussed with his neighbour such mundane matters as the depredations of cats.

He had few opportunities, for Captain Oring, that grey-bearded man who had dreamed for forty years of a shore life, was captain of a small tramp vessel which traded between London and Suez. He was not only captain but part proprietor, he and his sons holding three-quarters of the shares in this little vessel.

One of the "boys" was his chief officer, another his chief engineer, a third attended to the business end in London. He had, also, a daughter, a floridly-pretty girl, who kept the home for her brother and did an immense amount of housework in such time as she could spare from the pictures.

On an occasion when The Ringer was absent from London the girl disappeared. Her father was at sea, and it was from him, months later, that The Ringer heard the story.

Captain Oring did not tell him coherently—it was not the sort of story that a father could tell straightforwardly—and Henry Arthur Milton listened to the broken narrative with a cold-bloodedness which was his chief characteristic.

"My boy found her after a lot of trouble…she's with my sister now, in the country. Naturally, I've tried to find the people, but what chance have I got in London? I can't go to the police…. I don't want her name in the papers, do I? If I ever meet this man…."

"You won't," said The Ringer. "But perhaps I shall—I travel about a lot."

(In the neighbourhood he was registered as Mr. Ernest Oppenton, and his profession was described as "commercial traveller.")

Captain Oring went away to sea, with his sons and his grief and his patched-up little steamer; and Henry Arthur Milton had certain urgent business which took him to Berlin—so urgent that you might imagine that the matter of Lucy Oring had entirely slipped from his mind.

But nothing ever escaped him, and on his return to London he became a great frequenter of that type of West End club which appears on and is struck from the register so very rapidly that you might not know it had ever existed.

He overheard a little; waiters told him something. It is extraordinary how confidential an Italian waiter will become to a man who speaks his language. Women told him most of all, for he paid for drinks with great munificence.

On a certain afternoon a scene was enacted at one of the great London termini which was so commonplace that only very keen observation would have noted it as being out of the ordinary.

The nice-looking old lady with the white hair and the cameo brooch saw the train come slowly along the platform of Victoria Station, and moved nearer to the barrier.

Presently, the passengers began to trickle past the ticket-collector, not in the hurried way of suburban season-ticket holders, but with the leisure which is peculiar to travellers from a distance. She watched carefully, and after a while she saw the pretty girl with the black suitcase. She was dressed in dark brown and carried in her other hand a bunch of autumnal flowers.

The nice old lady intercepted her.

"My dear, are you Miss Clayford? I thought so! I am Mrs. Graddle. I thought I would come along and see you safely across London."

The girl nodded gratefully.

"I was wondering what I should do. Are you from the agency?"

The nice old lady smiled.

"Oh, dear no! But a friend of mine at the agency keeps me informed about the engagements. I like to do what I can for young people. Now, you must come along and have tea with me. I understand it is a perfectly awful place you are going to! Forty pounds a year for a nursery governess is scandalous! And in a little country village where there is nothing to see and nothing to do…!"

* * * *

She rattled on as she accompanied the girl through the booking-hall to the station yard, and Elsie Clayford listened dismally. Forty pounds a year was a small sum, but she understood that her new employers were very nice people, and that the home was comfortable. It was her first engagement.

"I'd like you to stay a few days with me," said Mrs. Graddle, as she signalled a cab. "I've got a lovely little house in St. John's Wood, and we have young society. I have already telephoned to Lady Shene, and she agrees. You might do a theatre or two…."

Elsie had not the vaguest idea who Mrs. Graddle was. She guessed that the old lady was a member of one of those organisations which undertake the care of young girls. It was a matter for satisfaction that such societies existed.

For instance, as she had met her white-haired guardian she had noticed a lank-looking man with long black hair and large horn-rimmed spectacles; and this sinister-looking individual had looked at her so oddly that she felt a queer little thrill of fear. And now he was standing at her elbow as the cab drew up at the kerb.

"Get in, my dear," said Mrs. Graddle, as Elsie pushed in her suitcase. The girl obeyed, and the old lady was following when the man with the spectacles caught her arm, and, drawing her gently aside, shut the cab door.

"King's Cross," he said to the driver, and, still holding Mrs. Graddle's arm, he pushed his head through the open window space. "Your train leaves at 5.32. Lady Shene will probably meet you at Welwyn Station. Have you money for the cab fare?"

"Ye-es," said the panic-stricken Elsie.

"Good. Don't talk to people unless you know them; especially angelic old birds like this one."

He waved the cab on.

"What's the idea?" demanded Mrs. Graddle, breathlessly.

The man had already called another cab.

"Get in," he said; and she obeyed tremblingly. The man followed.

"I've told him to drive through the park. I'll drop you at the end of Bird-cage Walk."

"I've a good mind to give you in charge!" There was a whimper in the old woman's voice. "Who do you think you are?" He did not answer this question.

"You've been convicted twice—once in Leeds and Manchester," he said; "and for a number of offences. You get acquainted with somebody in a registry office who keeps you supplied with information regarding the movement of servants. I understand that you're not above touting and using the cinemas to discover stage-struck girls."

"You can't prove anything," she interrupted. "And even if you arrest me —but you're not going to do a thing like that."

She opened her bag with trembling fingers, groped in the interior and took out a wad of bank-notes.

"Be a good man and don't make any trouble," she pleaded.

The Ringer took the notes from her hand, counted them deliberately.

"Sixty-five pounds doesn't seem a very adequate bribe," he remarked.

She opened an inner purse, and sorted out two notes, each for a hundred pounds.

"That's all I've got." Old Mrs. Graddle was inclined to be hysterical. "You busies' can't keep your noses out of anything!"

The Ringer tapped at the window and the cab stopped. It was now raining heavily, and there were few pedestrians about.

"Have you any children?" he asked.

"No," she said quickly.

"Apart from the beastliness of your job, do you ever realise what it feels like to be a father or a mother, to be waiting and hoping for somebody to come back…to be uncertain about their fate?"

"I don't want any argument with you," she said, with surprising savagery for so picturesque an old lady. "You've got your money, and that's all you care about! I've got no children."

"I think you're right," he said, cryptically; and opened the door for her.

"Let him drive on to the Tube station," she demanded; but he shook his head.

"You can get out and walk. You'll be wet through, probably, and die—and if you do I shan't stop laughing!"

She said something which no angelic old lady should have said. The Ringer smiled. As she moved quickly towards Parliament Square, he paid the cabman.

"Turn round and go back," he said, slipped on a mackintosh which he carried over his arm, took off his glasses, and wiped away his small moustache before the cabman had turned the nose of his machine in the other direction. He was taking no risks—the more so since he was well aware for what destination Mrs. Graddle was bound.

In the circumstances she went to a lot of unnecessary trouble in taking an Underground train to South Kensington and doubling back by taxi. Eventually she reached her pleasant home in St. John's Wood in a condition of semi-exhaustion.

It was a very nice house, with a beautiful dancing floor; this was necessary, for Mrs. Graddle gave select parties. The peculiar servants she employed were decorating the ballroom when she arrived, but she was not interested in the coming festivities of the evening.

* * * *

She went upstairs to the small study, where her son was eating greasy toast and reading the evening newspaper.

"Hullo! Did you get her?" he asked pleasantly.

He was a lethargic man of thirty, heavy-featured, heavy-eyed, and decidedly plump. On one finger he wore a diamond ring of great value; stones sparkled from his ornate cravat. He listened while she told her breathless story, stroking his small moustache.

"That's pretty bad," he said. "Who was he? Do you know him? A busy?' It's awkward—damned awkward! They know about the Leeds and the Manchester affair too; that's rotten!"

He had reason for his perturbation. Only by the skin of his teeth had he succeeded in keeping clear of the Manchester charge, and it would have been much more serious for him than for his mother.

"What are you scared about—I paid the feller, didn't I?" She rang the bell viciously, and when the servant came: "We shan't want the room for that girl; she's not coming," she snapped, and when the servant had closed the door: "For God's sake don't sit there shaking like a jelly, Julian! There's nothing to be afraid of!"

But Julian thought there were many things to be afraid of, and enumerated a few.

"I've been dreading this," he quavered, "ever since that Oring girl was found. Let's go down into the country, mother—what about Margate? We could stay there for a month or two till this affair blew over—"

"It has blown over," she interrupted, and went upstairs to change from her street clothes, which were most uncomfortably damp.

Julian Graddle never felt less like following his legitimate profession. He had to go into the West End to attend to two clients, for he was a ladies' hairdresser—an extremely useful trade to his mother: for women gossip to one another. They talk of servants who are leaving them, of girls who have got into scrapes. Some of his mother's best "finds" had been located by Julian in the course of his working day.

He was certainly not at his best after a series of sharp admonitions from his best client—a lady whose temper was by no means equable at the best of times, and he came to his second call more rattled than ever. The next day he had to attend at the shop which employed him, and he lived on tenterhooks, growing bolder, however, as the day progressed without a sign of a policeman.

In the evening, as he was leaving, the clerk at the desk handed him a slip of paper.

"Miss Smith, 34, Grine Mews, telephoned for you specially."

He frowned at the paper, but the time was convenient. "Six-thirty," said the note. "Miss Smith, very urgent. Pay on completion of work."

He was not at all surprised to be called to a mews. So many fashionable people had converted garages into artistic flats, and in the course of a normal week he made acquaintance with at least three.

The occupant of 34, Grine Mews, was obviously terminating her occupation. There was a board displayed, informing the world that "this handsome and commodious flat" was to let. He knocked at the narrow door, which was immediately opened.

"Come in," said a man's voice pleasantly. "Are you the hairdresser? Miss Smith has been waiting for you."

* * * *

Julian stumped wheezily up the steep stairs. They were uncarpeted, and so was the landing above. There was also the queer smell which attaches to houses that have been long unfurnished. Possibly Miss Smith was only just moving in, and was the victim of that enticing notice.

His conductor opened a door.

"This way. It is rather dark, but I'll get a light."

Julian entered unsuspectingly. The door slammed behind him—then there was a click, and a bare lamp hanging from the ceiling glowed dimly. The room was empty of furniture; the floor and mantelpiece were covered with dust. Over the little window a heavy horse-rug had been fastened with forks.

"Don't move," said the stranger.

His face was covered with a half-mask: a habit of The Ringer's when he was not wearing disguise.

"If you raise a bleat I shall shoot you through the stomach, and you will die in great agony," he said, calmly; and Julian's face went green at the sight of the pistol in the man's hand.

"What—what—?" he began.

"Don't ask questions. Go through that doorway."

Like a man in a dream, the prisoner obeyed. The inner room had a rickety table and a dark-coloured sofa, evidently left by a former tenant. On the table was a glass of red wine, and to this The Ringer pointed.

"Drink," he said, curtly.

The man turned an agonised face to him.

"Is it poisoned?" he whimpered.

"No, but I will tell you very frankly it is drugged. I'm not going to kill you—I promise you."

Julian gulped down the draught.

"Who are you?" he asked, hollowly.

"People call me The Ringer," said Henry Arthur Milton.

It was the last word Julian Graddle remembered.

* * * *

That night The Ringer had a long consultation with Captain Oring.

"He is the man all right, so we need not distress your daughter by bringing her up to identify him. Where is your ship lying?"

"She's lying at Keeney's Wharf, Rotherhithe," said Captain Oring, pondering the problem before him. "If I thought this was the man—"

"He is the man; but you're to do nothing drastic. He is to be kept alive and in good health. You will arrive at El Sass on the 23rd as I reckon the time—a day or two more or less doesn't matter, because you will be expected. You will arrange to hand him over at night to a crew of Arabs who will come out in a boat for him. Here is the money for his passage—two hundred and sixty-five pounds. His mother is paying the fare."

His two sons were with Captain Oring, and one of them spoke.

"If this is the man, Mr. Oppenton, we don't want any payment. I'd like to take the swine and beat his head off, but if you say no—well, your word goes."

What really was to happen to the man was explained before, in the middle of the night, they went down to the little garage at the end of the garden, where Mr. Julian Graddle was sleeping soundly, and bundled him into an old car. He was taken to Keeney's Wharf when the night watchman was dozing, and laid in a bumpy berth in a very uncomfortable little cabin....

To Ibn el Masjik The Ringer wrote a letter, and sent it overland by a series of aeroplane posts. It began:

> From his friend Arthur, to Ibn el Masjik, the servant of God, on whom be peace!
>
> I have thought much over the trouble which you confided to me, and of Certain Ones in your house who desire to follow the Western custom, making their hair short like men. Also, that you can find none in your city who may do this service for you.
>
> Now, El Masjik, I am sending to you a man very skilful in such things: a slave who has no protection of the law, and you shall keep him in your house all the days of his life, and I ask only that he be a servant to women, such an one as they may beat with their slippers.
>
> On the fourteenth day of the Month of the Pilgrimage a little steamer shall come to the port of El Sass and you shall send....

He gave the most minute instructions for the disposal of Mr. Julian Graddle—instructions that he knew would be obeyed to the letter.

A fortnight later he saw an advertisement in the agony columns of three daily newspapers:

> Will Julian Graddle, who disappeared from London, please communicate with his anxious and sorrowing mother?

And when he read this The Ringer laughed. He had read such appeals before, addressed by parents who sought daughters. And where those daughters had gone, and why they did not answer, the angelic Mrs. Graddle knew best.

Chapter 5

The Trimming of Paul Lumière

"It is not for me, sir, ever to say anything which suggests criticism," said Chief Inspector Mander with great diffidence: "the only thing I say is that possibly The Ringer has become too specialised a problem with you. You are, as it were, living too near to the subject."

Superintendent Bliss chewed on a quill toothpick thoughtfully. He disliked Mander extremely—but he was not singular in that.

Mander had very nice manners, spoke the King's English with a certain refinement of tone, looked well in evening dress, had fine company manners, and was suspected of employing his superiority in these respects to secure the rapid promotion which had come to him.

You searched his records without finding any great accomplishment. He had figured in a few unimportant cases, and had had charge of a murder—but the murderer had given himself up to justice, and had made a full confession to the local divisional inspector before Mander came on the scene; so there was no merit in that.

But he had, however, a wonderful knack of appearing clever to the right people. Bliss was not the right person. He never thought Mander was clever: invariably he referred to Inspector Mander in terms that were neither complimentary to the inspector nor commendable in himself.

Bliss was going to the south of France, partly on business, partly on holiday. He had not the slightest doubt in his mind what Mander was after; he had a malignant pleasure in the thought that, if there was one man at Scotland Yard to whom he would like to hand over The Ringer case it was Mr. Mander, he of the aristocratic nose and the fair moustache.

"All right—take control while I am away. I'll arrange for my clerk to turn over anything that comes. It isn't going to be an easy job for you."

"So you have found," said Mander, with a smile.

"So *you* will find, inspector," replied Bliss emphatically.

He had not left London before he saw in the columns of a daily newspaper that "Chief Inspector Mander had assumed control of The Ringer case during the absence of Superintendent Bliss."

Mander was strong on publicity.

On the following day a letter arrived at Scotland Yard. It was addressed to Superintendent Bliss, and those who were in the habit of handling his correspondence had no doubt as to who was the writer.

"The Ringer? Rubbish! Why does he write? Does he write to Bliss?"

The man took the letter with a contemptuous smile and tore open the envelope. The letter was written on just that coloured paper which The Ringer invariably used.

> Mr. Paul Lumière is a man for whom I have no affection. He began life as a common thief; he is a sweater of labour, a trickster; and he once treated a friend of mine very badly—not so badly that he deserves the shades, but badly enough to deserve robbing.
>
> I purpose taking from him the sum of £30,000—or its equivalent. This will be the price offered to Randwell and Coles, the Bond Street jewellers, for a diamond and emerald chain. After the chain has been acquired by its purchaser it will be acquired by me.

"Who is Paul Lumière?" demanded Mander. His immediate subordinate went forth to make inquiries. There was, he discovered, no Paul Lumière in any of the available directories.

"Sheer braggadocio!" said Mr. Mander, who had a line of classy words. "I suppose this is the sort of thing that impresses Bliss."

"Whenever The Ringer sends that kind of letter he follows it up with a *coup*," warned the sergeant.

Mr. Mander made derisive noises.

He was working in his office that night when the sergeant, who had gone off duty hours before, walked into his room.

"I've found Paul Lumière," he said; and, producing an evening newspaper from his pocket, he pointed to a paragraph which he had marked:

> Mr. Paul Lumière, the American millionaire, who arrived from New York last week, is buying Old Masters for his private gallery, and yesterday bought a lovely example of the early Flemish school for a thousand guineas from Messrs. Theimer, of Grafton Street.

Mander was instantly alert.

"Get on to the principal hotels, and find out where he is staying."

It was not difficult to locate Mr. Lumière. He had a suite in London's most crowded hotel. When Mander put through a call he found that the millionaire, who went early to bed, had retired to his room, and was not to be disturbed. Nor, when Mander made a personal call, did he have any greater success.

* * * *

He decided to call the next morning, but before he made his visit he dropped in at the Bond Street jeweller's whose name had been mentioned in the letter.

The head of the firm was in the south of France, and he saw the managing director.

"Mr. Paul Lumière? Oh, yes. We have had some negotiations with him. He is buying some jewellery from us—the Alexandriff necklace, to be exact." And then, suspiciously: "Is there anything wrong about him?"

"Oh, nothing, nothing!" said Mander, impatiently. Like all men of his peculiar mentality, he resented being asked questions. "He is all right—a millionaire or something. I am merely looking after his interests. I don't mind telling you—I shall probably have to tell you later, in any case—that an attempt is being made to rob him; and I want you, when the time comes, to afford me all the assistance you possibly can."

The managing director was naturally curious, but Inspector Mander was not in the mood to satisfy that curiosity.

He called in at Scotland Yard to look through his letters before going on to the Revoy Hotel, and found that Mr. Paul Lumière had made matters very easy.

There was a note from him, enclosing a letter of introduction. It bore the printed letter-head of Police Headquarters in New York City.

Dear Sir,
    May I personally commend to your care Mr. Paul Lumière, of this city? Mr. Lumière, who is going to Europe, has for some months past been the recipient of threatening letters from The Ringer. There may be nothing to this, but I happen to know that Mr. Lumière has, for some reason or other, incurred the animosity of this man. Will you be good enough to give Mr. Lumière any assistance he may require?
    Sincerely,
                                                            E. B. Sullivan.

The covering note was a formal invitation asking Bliss to call, and a few minutes after reading these epistles Inspector Mander was shown into the millionaire's suite.

Mr. Lumière was a tall, not ill-looking man, with a short, grey moustache and a mop of iron grey hair. He had a nervous little trick of screwing up his mouth every few seconds, but apparently this was no evidence of any apprehension so far as The Ringer was concerned.

"Sit right down, captain—I'm glad to know you. Say, who is this bird, The Ringer? Milton, eh? Never met him, but I'm not scared—no, sir...." He talked rapidly, continuously. Mr. Mander, who was not averse from hearing himself talk, waited impatiently for the opportunity.

He received the impression that The Ringer and the cause of his vendetta was not unknown to Mr. Lumière. Once or twice the millionaire referred vaguely to "this girl Fleitcher," but who "this girl Fleitcher" was he did not explain.

"The only thing I know," said Mander, "is that he has threatened to rob you. He says that you are buying jewellery to the value of thirty thousand pounds—"

Lumière's jaw dropped.

"Well, I'll be damned, the Alexandriff necklace! A hundred and fifty thousand dollars. Now, how in hell did he know that?"

* * * *

Mr. Mander was not in a position to answer the inquiry.

"I want you to do me this favour: Whenever you go to Randwell and Coles ring me up and I will go with you. If you take money—"

"Am I crazy?" demanded the other, contemptuously. "I'll pay with a banker's draft if I pay at all. But I'll certainly tip you off when the negotiations reach that point. What do you think of that picture—?"

For the next ten minutes he talked of his recent purchases—the sitting-room was littered with works of art that he had been offered or had bought.

Mr. Mander returned to his office with a fixed smile. For once in his life The Ringer had made a mistake. He had a different type of man to deal with from Bliss.

Bliss was tired, lived too near the problem of The Ringer to adjust himself instantly to every new development. A fresh brain, a fresh outlook, and methods which, Mr. Mander flattered himself, were a little out of the ordinary, would produce results for which Superintendent Bliss had groped in vain.

In his exhilaration, he sat down and wrote a long letter to the absent superintendent, telling him just how the case was developing, and giving him a bare outline of the measures he was taking to meet and defeat the machinations of Henry Arthur Milton.

Naturally, I shall take no chances (he wrote). Lumière has promised that in no circumstances will he make the purchase without notifying me.

He made a second call upon Randwell and Coles, and had a long conference with the manager.

"You understand that when Mr. Lumière buys this necklace it is to be taken by two trustworthy assistants to him at the hotel. In no circumstances must he buy it here and take it away with him. I will arrange that you have four of the best men from Scotland Yard to escort your salesmen. It would be better, perhaps, if you came yourself to take the banker's draft. You can have the detectives to guard you back to Bond Street."

The manager laughed.

"A banker's draft wouldn't be of much use to The Ringer," he said; and then: "Perhaps you would like to see the article which Mr. Lumière is trying to buy. We're asking thirty-five thousand, but I think the purchase price will be nearer thirty; naturally, we're after the best price we can get, but he's a very shrewd man and knows more about precious stones than most people I have met."

He unlocked a safe in his private office and took out a tray on which lay a long and dazzling chain of diamonds and emeralds.

"Some of these stones weigh eight carats. Those three emeralds"—he pointed with his little finger—"are worth something like £5,000 in the open market. As a matter of fact, we get very little profit, because the value of this chain, which came to us from Russia, is in the stones and not in the setting."

* * * *

Mander interviewed the Assistant Commissioner and gave him particulars of the steps he had taken to safeguard the chain.

"It comes down to a question of system," he graciously explained. "I am a great admirer of the work of Superintendent Bliss, but it has always struck me as being a little haphazard, and left open all sorts of avenues of escape.

"In this case I purpose, if you have no objection, utilising the full strength of the Yard. I shall have the hotel surrounded by detectives; I shall have men in every corridor; and if The Ringer can get in or out he will be a much cleverer man than I gave him credit for."

The Assistant Commissioner, who had a very high regard for the genius of Bliss, listened coldly.

"One thing you must be careful about, inspector, is a possible confederate—probably a woman," he said. "The Ringer is a quick and efficient worker."

Mr. Mander smiled.

"I also have some sort of reputation, sir," he said; and the Assistant Commissioner was too polite to ask for particulars.

Mander, in his way, was very thorough. He took a census of every room occupied at the hotel and paid particular attention to the guests whose rooms were adjacent to Mr. Lumière's suite. The room adjoining Lumière's own bedroom was occupied by a Miss Gwerth Stacey, who had arrived at the hotel on the same day as Lumière. She was an American and a physical culture expert. Lumière, who confessed that he had had several chats with her, said she was a fanatic on the question of hotel fires.

She told him that she never went into an hotel without making a survey of her position and discovering the quickest way of leaving the building—a

48

quite unnecessary precaution so far as the Revoy Hotel was concerned, for in every room there was a fire alarm.

"Trail her up," said Mander to one of his subordinates. "She's the most suspicious-looking individual in the hotel."

All the trailing, however, revealed no more than that she attended lectures on hygiene and physical culture which were being delivered at that period by a Swedish authority. She had apparently one or two professional friends in London with whom she occasionally went to supper and a dance.

But Mander was taking no risks: he instructed a woman detective to make this athletic young lady her especial care. He chose the five best detectives at the Yard and gave them detailed instructions as to what they were to do in certain emergencies, and, in addition, earmarked four reliable men to accompany the jeweller to the hotel.

That pilgrimage of commerce came on the very day he completed his arrangements. A telephone message brought him to the jewellers' and he interviewed the managing director in his private office.

"We have agreed to a price, and Mr. Lumière is taking possession of the chain this afternoon at half-past four."

That was all Mander wanted to know.

He put into movement the machinery he had created to circumvent Scotland Yard's cleverest and chiefest enemy. Plain-clothes officers were detailed to watch every railway terminus: a corps of watchers was distributed about the hotel; and at four o'clock, when the jewellers' manager stepped into a car that waited in Bond Street, four stalwart detectives closed in on and entered the machine with him.

At the entrance to the hotel were two police officers in uniform. In the corridor on Mr. Lumière's floor two detectives, Mander's most reliable officers, were awaiting them.

The inspector was with Mr. Lumière when the treasure arrived, and the millionaire chuckled as he saw this unusually large party crowd into the room.

"Lock the door," said Mander, authoritatively, and his order was carried out.

The jeweller took a case from his inside pocket, laid it on the table, and opened the cover. Under the overhead light of the glass chandelier the beautiful rope flashed into a thousand hues.

"You've got a bargain, Mr. Lumière," said the manager.

The purchaser shrugged his shoulders.

"I'm not so sure that it's a great bargain," he said, good-humouredly. "At any rate, you have your money."

He took a banker's draft from his pocket and handed it to the jeweller, who examined it carefully and slipped it into his pocket-case.

49

"What do you intend doing with this piece of jewellery?" asked Mander. "I presume you're going to put it into the hotel safe?"

* * * *

Mr. Lumière smiled and shook his head.

"I've something more secure than any hotel safe in my room," he said. "Nobody knows about it but myself, and I can only assure you that I will put it in a place that not even you and your detectives could find."

Mander frowned at this.

"Why not—" he began.

"My friend," said Mr. Lumière, quietly, "I trust nobody! If you do not know where I have placed it, and none of your intelligent officers—one of whom may be The Ringer for all I know—sees where it goes, I have only myself to blame if it is lost."

He took up the case, walked quickly into his bedroom, and closed the door. The jeweller looked at the detective and chuckled.

"I shouldn't be surprised if he's right," he said. "These people who are in the habit of carrying stones are very seldom robbed."

Mander was in something of a quandary; he had no authority to demand that he should be shown where the jewels were hidden, and the suggestion which was thrown out by Lumière that one of his men might possibly be The Ringer gave him a moment's uneasiness. He was so impressed that he had them lined up and looked closely at one after the other. They were clean-shaven, and none bore the slightest resemblance to the description he had had of this notable individual.

"I suppose it's all right—" he began.

And then he heard a cry in the corridor outside, and a quick scamper of feet. Instantly he was outside the door, in time to see a woman flying along the corridor, pursued by the two detectives. She turned an angle of the wall, and fled to the stairs.

Mander dashed back into the room and tried the door of Lumière's bedroom; it was locked.

"Are you there...Mr. Lumière?"

He tapped on the panel, but there was no answer. He shouted again, and then flung all his weight against the door. The lock was a stout one, and did not budge.

"Come here, two of you fellows!" he shouted, savagely; and two of the heaviest detectives applied their shoulders to the door. There was a crack, and a crash, and the door flew open.

The room was empty. It was a large bedroom, from which led two other doors, one apparently into the bathroom and the other to the corridor. This, they found, was unlocked. There was no sign of Lumière, nor of the diamond rope.

The windows were fastened, and exit from here would have been almost impossible, for the suite was on the fourth floor, and there was a sheer drop; and there was no means by which even a cat could have climbed down.

Mander's face was very pale. He realised that something had happened, something that might be very unpleasant to himself. He rushed into the corridor in time to see the two detectives bringing back a protesting and dishevelled young lady, whom he recognised as Miss Stacey.

She was incoherent with wrath. It was a long time before she could make any understandable statement.

* * * *

"Now come across, my girl—you were working with The Ringer," said Mander, when he had taken the girl into the sitting-room. "He handed you the stuff and you bolted with it—where is Mr. Lumière?"

"Are you crazy?" she demanded, shrilly. "Who is The Ringer, anyway? The fire-bell went, and I ran downstairs. Just as I had got to the hall, these two...."

* * * *

Mander looked at her incredulously.

"Fire-bell?" he said. "There's been no fire alarm."

"The fire-bell went, I tell you," she insisted, "and the indicator dropped, and the red light burnt."

He followed her into her room and discovered that she had spoken only the truth. The bell was still ringing; a red light glowed at the side, and the indicator which dropped at the ringing of the bell showed plainly.

He returned to Lumière's room, stunned with amazement. By this time the hotel staff had gathered. Nobody had seen any sign of Mr. Lumière.

"What is that door?" He pointed to a plain door opposite the bedroom of the missing man.

"That is the baggage lift," said the valet.

Mander made his way quickly down the stairs to the hall. His policemen were still on guard at the door, but they had seen no sign of the missing millionaire.

He was about to turn into the manager's office when he heard a well-remembered and much-disliked voice.

"Have you lost him?"

He spun round on his heels, to meet the unpleasant smile of Superintendent Bliss.

"I came back this afternoon, after I had your letter," said Bliss, in his deliberate way. "I gather you've had some trouble?"

51

By this time Mander was nearly hysterical.

"I've had no trouble," he almost shouted. "I took every precaution. I have had every entrance guarded—"

"Go back to the Yard and leave this case to me, will you?" said Bliss.

* * * *

It was late that night when a miserable detective inspector was summoned to his superintendent's office. He found Bliss chewing at a half-smoked cigar.

"Sit down, Mr. Mander." Bliss's voice was icily polite. "In the first place," he said, "let me explain why I came back from Nice. When I got your letter I pretty well knew that The Ringer was purposely taking advantage of your innocence. He knew I'd left London—you saw to that! And when he addressed the letter to Bliss he knew very well that Mr. Mander would open it.

"It was the cleverest little *coup* that he'd ever planned, and I've not the slightest doubt—this may bring a little comfort to you—that he would have tried it on me, and possibly have succeeded. Do you know the firm of Randwell and Coles?"

"I know they are jewellers, that is all," said Mander, unhappily.

"Randwell and Coles," said Bliss, "are names which cover the identity of a very rich man who changed his name some years ago to Chapman. It was previously Lumière, and when The Ringer told you that he was going to rob Lumière, that was the Lumière that he meant."

"And who was the other Lumière?"

He saw Bliss smile, and his jaw dropped.

"The Ringer?" he squeaked.

Bliss nodded.

"The millionaire in his suite at the Revoy was our dear friend. To get possession of the thirty thousand pound necklace was a very simple matter, with a forged bank draft, always supposing that he could find a mug at Scotland Yard who would vouch for him. He found one. You left the unfortunate jewellers no doubt as to the bona fides of Mr. Lumière. If you had cabled to New York, to Mr. Sullivan, of the police department, you would have discovered that Mr. Sullivan died last year; and if you had ever seen a letter-head from Police Headquarters at New York you would also have known that the heading of the letter you received was printed in London.

"As to the fire alarm—I'm not so sure that that wasn't as clever as anything The Ringer has ever attempted. He knew all about this girl who was living next door; knew exactly her horror of fires, and she served him rather well, because at the psychological moment, by inserting a steel needle through the plaster of the wall and short-circuiting the fire alarm, he was able to send that timorous female flying for her life with the two people who had been set to watch the passage running after her.

"That gave him the opportunity he wanted. He slipped into the luggage lift, went down into the basement; he had his quick-change ready, and was out through the service entrance before you could say 'knife!'"

Mr. Mander said nothing.

"The Ringer isn't easy, is he?" asked Bliss, maliciously.

Chapter 6

The Blackmail Boomerang

There was a man who had an office in Chancery Lane, who described himself as The Exsome Domestic Agency. His ostensible business was the placing of good-class domestic servants in new situations, and he specialised in that type of servant who had reason for not applying to his or her late employer for the indispensable "character."

He did not advertise this fact, either in the newspapers or on his nice note-heading, but it was pretty well known that he would supply necessary credentials for a consideration.

> This man (or woman) we know to have been employed by Mr.
> Hackitt, who is now in India. Mr. Hackitt left England in a hurry, but
> in a letter to us he spoke in the highest possible terms of....

Mr. Exsome was very friendly with his clients. He would talk to them, drink with them, and sometimes learn important facts. Mr. Exsome had another agency which called itself the Secret Service Bureau. In this capacity he was a private detective, and, as such, would call upon the late employers of his servant clients.

Was it true that Mrs. Z—had once entertained Mr. Y—in the absence of her husband? Was she aware that there was a blackmailer trying to make capital out of the knowledge? And would she leave everything in the hands of the Secret Service Bureau—at a fee to be settled later?

Mrs. Z—, in a panic would agree, and from time to time would pay the exorbitant fees of her "protector." In this way "Skid" Exsome made a very large income.

His intimate associates called him "Skid" because he had the knack of side-slipping most of the dangers that came his way.

He had a lovely house near Egham, a flat in Maida Vale, and ran the most expensive of cars. For these luxuries two people had paid with their lives. (Mrs. Albany's suicide will be remembered) and hundreds had paid in cash. To build his own house he had broken many; to provide for the jewels with which his phlegmatic wife bedecked herself many jewels had been sold and many little properties mortgaged.

Mr. Exsome had never been convicted—he had "skidded" most effectively.

Mrs. Leadale Verriner once employed a butler who vanished one morning with the contents of her jewel-case. She was out hunting at the time, and returned to find her flimsy safe ripped open and property to the value of £3,000 gone. It was not until after she had communicated with the police that she remembered that there were other things in the case besides jewellery.

She did not go grey or haggard. She was a sane and wise as well as a pretty woman. She went to Scotland Yard and interviewed Bliss and told him all about Bobbie, who was now in India, and about her grumbling, difficult and jealous husband. She did not tell Mr. Bliss very much about the letters that Bobbie had written; but the superintendent was a man of the world and a good guesser.

When the butler was arrested he was interviewed at Scotland Yard. Most of the jewellery had been disposed of; the letters, he said glibly, he had destroyed. "Threw them into the fire," was his explanation.

"I hope you did, Cully," said Bliss, who knew the butler's record rather well. "You'll get five for this job; but if, when you come out, you put the black on this lady I'll undertake to get you another fourteen."

"If I drop dead this minute," said Cully virtuously, "I burnt them letters."

He did not drop dead that minute, proving beyond any doubt whatever that Providence gives a miss to the most tempting invitations.

Cully got a three, and, coming out, looked for another job. The Exsome Agency was pretty well known in Dartmoor, and to Mr. Exsome he went. That gentleman also knew Cully's record and treated him most kindly. In the course of a couple of lunches, and an evening spent at a music-hall and worse, Cully made mysterious references to letters.

The next day he brought them to the office and "Skid" read them very carefully. He checked up Mrs. Leadale Verriner's social and financial position, discovered that she had an income of her own of two thousand a year, and that her husband was even better off.

He bought the letters, after some bargaining, for £320, and they immediately came within the operations of the Secret Service Bureau....

Mrs. Verriner listened without comment to the apologetic "detective" who called upon her.

"No, it isn't your late butler," said Mr. Exsome. "I've taken a great deal of trouble to seek out that unfortunate man. He told me he threw them away, at a spot where the man who has approached me found them."

She was a little haggard now, possibly because Bobbie was married, and had written long, incoherent, rather foolish letters explaining his treachery and how everything was for the best.

Mr. Exsome waited for her to speak and then went on: "This man wishes to get to Australia and start life afresh—"

"It is a very common excuse, isn't it?" she asked coldly, and Mr. Exsome knew that she was going to be very difficult—the kind of woman who would go to the police if she was not handled rightly. He proceeded to handle her rightly.

He rose from his chair with a certain brusqueness.

"Well, madam, I've done all I possibly can, and there the matter ends so far as I am concerned. This blundering fool of a man may very well approach your husband, though why he should I don't know. But, as I say, these people are perfect fools—"

She signalled him to sit down again, and thenceforward she began to pay and pay, and one by one the letters were returned to her—all except the only one that counted.

On the loneliest corner of her pretty little Berkshire estate was a small cottage, rented by a French artist, who spent occasional weekends at the place. He kept no servants, for the simple reason that his language could not be understood.

Mrs. Verriner had had one or two talks with this long-haired gentleman with the twirling black moustache, and in his florid, extravagant way, he had placed his demesne—which cost him a pound a week—at her disposal.

Soon after Mr. Exsome began to draw on his new source of revenue she took the Frenchman at his word—to his undisguised amazement.

"I have people coming to see me whom I don't wish to receive at the house," she said. "It would be very convenient, Monsieur Vaux, if I could tell them to come here. Naturally, I would arrange these meetings while you were away."

"Why, *certainement!*" smiled her tenant. "When I am in residence I will elevate to this little flagpole a small tricolour. Madam, I place in your hands the key of my little château!"

When the flagstaff was bare she strolled across to the cottage, unlocked the back door, and in the very plain sitting-room furnished with sketches, finished and unfinished, she listened to Mr. Exsome's newest explanation.

* * * *

On a balmy spring evening Mr. Exsome was smoking a fragrant cigar in his Maida Vale flat. The letter came by hand, which puzzled him. It was typewritten and bore a typewritten signature:

> I have discovered that you are a professional blackmailer. I do not like blackmailers, professional or amateur. Find another occupation. I shall not warn you again.

The typewritten signature was "The Ringer," and Mr. Exsome's jaw dropped, for just then the newspapers were full of the recent exploits of that criminal.

His complacent wife came in soon after.

"Why, Ernie, you're looking very pale. What's the matter?" she asked. "Got your income tax assessment—"

She could be heavily jocular.

"Shut up!" he snarled.

Now, even he knew that it would take a big skid to avoid The Ringer; but he was on a good thing in Mrs. Leadale Verriner, had indeed only touched the edge of her resources. In a foolish moment of confidence, she had told him she would be very rich when her uncle died, and her uncle, as Mr. Exsome had already discovered, was nearer to eighty than seventy. This time he was out for big money, and it looked reasonable odds on his getting what he wished. As for The Ringer—

Going out that evening to the car that waited at the door, he saw a newspaper boy who carried an amazingly cheering poster: "The Ringer Located."

He bought a paper, his hand so trembling that he could hardly see the print; presently he found the item and learnt little except what he had discovered on the poster.

* * * *

Once upon a time a certain unpleasant gentleman was consigned by The Ringer to a hot little town set in the wastes of the Arabian desert, for offences which need not be particularised. And there for three months he performed the office of hairdresser and head shingler to the women of one Ibn el Masjik.

One day he conceived the idea of setting forth the story of his wrongs in a long, long letter to the Foreign Minister of Great Britain, and, by bribery and corruption, persuaded a camel-driver named The Accursed (for some ancient sin of his forefathers) to carry the letter to a civilised place. He also wrote to his mother, but that letter was lost the night our accursed camel-driver got drunk in Benarim and the unveiled women with whom he was spending the evening went through his turban in the hope of finding enough money to pay them for the trouble of throwing him out of the window.

The letter reached Whitehall and was sent across to Scotland Yard. Inspector Bliss was hardly stirred by the fate of Mr. Julian Graddle, but he was tremendously interested in certain sequences of cause and effect. Somebody had been indiscreet; a wronged father (who was also a seagoing captain and Mr. Graddle's custodian) had spoken highly of his neighbour who had engineered the kidnapping.

Bliss had something to go on. A police tender raided a house in Norbury. The Ringer escaped by the back door of a tiny garage as the tender halted at the corner of the street. He was in his respectable car with a heavy red moustache and a heavier pipe; he passed Bliss, and the superintendent did not give him more than a glance.

That evening every private police wire radiating from the instrument room at Scotland Yard carried the duplication of this message:

> Very urgent; very urgent. Hold brown Buick two-seater T.D. 7418. Seen ten minutes ago Great West Road stop Staines report Slough report Maidenhead report Reading report stop Arrest and detain driver of car stop Dangerous carries firearms stop Report Bliss Scotland Yard.

"I think," said Inspector Mander, fingering his fair moustache, "that this is where we get him."

A buoyant soul was Inspector Mander. Failure was so normal a condition that a very recent and flagrant misfire of his, which would have crushed most men, had not more than momentarily depressed him.

Superintendent Bliss regarded him with an unfriendly eye.

"You will be interested to learn that the car has been discovered in Epping Forest, which is exactly the opposite direction to that in which he was seen moving. And if you want an afternoon's occupation you will probably work out the route he followed. I have already done so, but you are so much cleverer than I that you may be able to show me a point."

* * * *

The next clue Scotland Yard received was from the Berkshire police. There was, apparently, living on the estate of Mrs. Leadale Verriner, a French artist who occupied his bungalow only during the weekend. In his absence, as he learnt when he returned rather earlier than usual, some unauthorised person had been living in the bungalow and had been sleeping in a room which the artist did not use. He left behind a small map on which two routes were traced in red ink, one leading to the south of England and one —and this explained the disposition of the car—through Hounslow, Hampton, and by a circuitous route to North London.

"I'd better go down and see this Frenchman and have a look at the cottage," suggested Mander.

"Do you speak French?" asked his chief, coldly.

"No, sir, but I can make myself understood—"

"The question is whether he'll make himself understood. Leave him to the Berkshire police."

Mrs. Leadale Verriner got to know of the burglary from her tenant, and at first she was a little alarmed.

"I will tell you the truth, my dear madam. At first I said nothing because I thought it was your friend! You are a lady; I have placed my house at your disposition. What is more likely than that you should say: 'Very good, you shall sleep here tonight. I am sure my friend Mr. Vaux would not object.' And would I object, madam? Most assuredly I would not!

"But when I hear of this Ringer, I say, 'Ha, ha!' I do not fear this Ringer —I snap my fingers at him and say 'Pff!' I search the little room and what do I discover? The map. This, I think, is strange. And then I find a revolver —I do not tell the police about that! I think I will keep that revolver for my-self, though I am not nervous truly! But it is a souvenir. And then I find you have been away in London, so your friend could not have been here, and I speak to the police."

She bit her lip thoughtfully. She was growing rather peaked; there were dark shadows under her eyes. She had been to London to negotiate a mort-gage on a house she owned in Wiltshire. And her husband was growing sus-picious—an easy process—of the real cause for her clandestine meetings with Mr. Exsome in the artist's cottage.

"You don't think he came—while my friend was here, that he was in the house all the time?"

He shook his head and smiled.

"He would not be so ungallant," he said, so archly that she stiffened.

* * * *

Exsome was growing more and more requiring. The few hundreds that were to send the unknown owner of the letters to Australia had been suc-ceeded by a demand for a thousand. Her husband's present suspicion was but a foretaste of the attitude he would adopt if the letters ever came to his notice. She had got to the point where she could not sleep; she was making her last desperate effort to satisfy the rapacity which Mr. Exsome inter-preted in terms more suave.

Exsome waited patiently. He knew to the minute when to put on the screw and when to release it. Frantic letters were coming to him from his victim telling him the progress she was making in the rather protracted ne-gotiations which were going on between herself and a lawyer. Early one af-ternoon he received a wire:

Meet cottage eight o'clock. Bring letters. Cash ready.

It was a large sum he had demanded—the ultimate squeeze. Thereafter any further demands would drive her to Scotland Yard, and Mr. Exsome knew just where to stop.

He got the letter out of his safe, put it in his pocket, and was on the point of going to the little club in Soho, where one can bet race by race, when an urgent telephone call came through for him.

* * * *

There are more than eighteen thousand constables in the Metropolitan Police Force, and it would be very remarkable if there were not one or two crooks among them. One of these had been fired out of Scotland Yard for malpractice, but had kept in touch, through a friend, with a great deal that was happening at police headquarters, and he was a very useful servant to Mr. Exsome.

"It's Joe," said the voice, and when Joe spoke in a tone so urgent that his voice was almost unrecognisable, Mr. Exsome sat up and took notice.

"Anything wrong?" he asked quickly.

"I've just had it straight," said the speaker rapidly. "Bliss has got an information against you. Somebody's raised a squeak—name of Lynn."

Mr. Exsome nodded. He remembered the Lynn case—the son of a wealthy member of the Stock Exchange who had got himself into very serious trouble and had, in consequence, enriched Mr. Exsome's treasury to an incredible amount.

"Is there a warrant?" he asked.

"There will be tomorrow. You'll be under observation from tonight."

"Thank you, Joe," said Mr. Exsome gratefully.

He was prepared for such a crisis. His bank was only a few doors from the flat in which he lived. He arrived there twenty minutes before closing time, and drew so substantially upon his balance that the manager had to be sent for to make delivery from the private vault.

He went back and saw his wife. She had a private account of her own and needed no provision.

"I shall be away for a few months," he said, and she accepted his hasty departure philosophically.

He read the telegram again. He would go by train to Windsor, taking his bicycle, would cross Windsor Great Park, and reach the cottage in the twilight. The bicycle would get him to Slough and the main Western line... there was a boat leaving Plymouth for a French port that night. By the time the warrant was issued he would be well away.

Everything worked according to plan. He rode at his leisure through the deserted park, and came to the cottage a quarter of an hour before the time of his appointment. There was nobody in sight on the road. He passed through the garden gate and made a circuit of the house. Near the hedge which separated the artist's little garden from the park somebody had been digging. A deep trench had been cut—he was only faintly interested in this.

He pushed at the back door—it was open. So the lady had arrived! He left his bicycle against the wall and entered, closing the door softly behind him. The door of the sitting-room was ajar, and a light was burning.

"Well, madam——" he began cheerfully as he entered.

"Shut the door," said the pleasant-faced man who was sitting at the other side of the table.

* * * *

Mr. Exsome stopped and stared.

"You don't know me?" The stranger smiled. "You'll be interested to learn that you're one of the few people who have ever seen The Ringer without his make-up."

"The Ringer?" croaked Exsome, and his face went green.

"Don't run—I can shoot quicker than you can move."

His right hand was caressing a Browning.

"Won't you sit down?"

The blackmailer sank back into a chair. He was speechless, could only gape at Judgment.

"You've had a fair warning, I think?" He asked the question in a pleasant, conversational tone. "I've been on your trail for quite a long time, but you've been so clever that it's been a little difficult to identify you, and I've been rather busy myself lately," he smiled. "And then I happened to be staying here. I've got one or two little bolt-holes, you know—they're rather necessary."

"When Mrs. Verriner said she had a friend to meet I feared the worst; but, then, I'm not a censor of morals. Curiosity and interest induced me to stay in the house one day when you came—you never know what you may learn of value if you listen hard enough. Of course, I am so much of a gentleman that if it had been a vulgar love affair I shouldn't have listened at all. But it wasn't a vulgar love affair; it was a vulgar blackmailing affair. Did you bring the letter?"

Exsome nodded dumbly.

"Put it on the table. Throw on to the table also the money you drew from the bank. I phoned you this afternoon and got you on the run—oh! yes, I know all about Joe; that was only natural, for I made a very thorough inquiry about you and your connections."

He waited a little while, and then said sharply, "The letter and the money!"

Exsome obeyed; and then he found his voice.

"Is that all you want?" he asked huskily.

The Ringer shook his head.

"I want something more. I've been looking up your cases. I don't suppose you ever think of them—they're not nice, are they? Do you remember that unfortunate lady who was found with her head in a gas oven? And the girl who walked into a pond and stayed there? And that elderly clergyman who went a little wrong in his head after you'd taken sixteen hundred pounds out of him? Now, take only those few cases."

Mr. Exsome remembered them rather well. The memory of them was very vivid at that moment. Perhaps for the first time he was seeing another point of view.

"That's all," said The Ringer, and rose. "Let's go outside."

* * * *

The morning mail brought Mrs. Leadale Verriner two letters—one from the lawyer regretting his inability to arrange the mortgage; the other (and this was registered) a letter three years old, and she nearly fainted.

With it was a slip of paper which said:

I shall not trouble you again. All the money I received from you I have paid into your London account.

Bewildered, yet half swooning with joy, she pushed the letter into the grate.

Ten minutes later her banker rang her. The money had arrived by post.

"Only your name written on a postcard was with the bank-notes."

Her husband was in town. That afternoon she saw the tricolour flying and strolled across to the cottage. The Frenchman was in his garden, a long cheroot between his teeth, and he greeted her volubly.

"Here is your key, Monsieur Vaux," she said in her excellent French. And then, with a smile: "You were very busy yesterday afternoon. One of my keepers told me he saw you digging frantically!"

She looked round the garden; there was no sign of the trench the gamekeeper had reported, but the earth had been turned and a new oval garden-bed had appeared amid the rank grass.

"There I shall plant forget-me-nots," said Mr. Vaux, "which shall remind you of one small service which I was able to render you, madam."

She thought he was referring to the key. He was, in point of fact, thinking of something quite different.

62

Chapter 7

Miss Brown's £7,000 Windfall

Mr. Gilbert Orsan was an industrious writer: he might not, perhaps, rival that inventor of tales who, if rumour does not lie, produces a novel a week and a play a fortnight. And he certainly could not be credited with the fabulous income of that restless man; for Mr. Orsan was not paid for his contributions to journalism. He wrote letters on genealogy and the thriftlessness of the poor, and similar cheerful subjects.

As to the thriftlessness of the poor, he might claim to be an authority. The rents due to him were sometimes, on the aggregate, as much as a thousand pounds in arrears. He owned a very considerable amount of house property in the south, east, north, and west of London.

Sometimes the most unpleasant things were said about him—both as landlord and employer. For he was also the proprietor of the Orsan Stores, which had branches in every part of the metropolis. He invariably wrote about these outcries against his humanity as "carefully engineered." He referred to them as "artificial grievances," and put them down to "the unscrupulous agitations of Communists."

Communism was a great blessing to Mr. Orsan. He ascribed all criticism to the "growing spirit of lawlessness engendered by the pestiferous doctrines of Moscow."

Yet, if the truth be told, there were thousands of people who hated Moscow and Mr. Orsan with equal ferocity.

Lila Brown should have been one of these, but she was too sore at heart to hate any but herself.

Yet Mr. Orsan had behaved very generously to her. As he said in his godlike way, These Things Happen, and there was no sense in Making Mountains out of Molehills. She ceased to be Mr. Orsan's housekeeper-secretary and went to live at Schofield's boarding-house at Hythe, on four pounds a week, which was little enough to keep two people, even though one of the two lived on an exclusive diet of milk and patent barley.

* * * *

63

A quiet man went to live at Schofield's. He was of uncertain age, rather good-looking, and his hair was greyish at the temples. He had one trick of inviting and inspiring confidence, and another of making people talk about things that they could never dream they would ever discuss with their nearest friends. And he loved babies, and handled them beautifully—he had once "walked" an Edinburgh hospital.

So, in the course of the quiet weeks when Superintendent Bliss was seeking him in every part of England except Hythe, the engaging man learned all about Mr. Orsan and his *ménage*, and the little passage that led from the garage to the study, which Mr. Orsan used when he took friends to the house who could not go more openly without endangering his reputation for sanctity.

And Miss Brown showed him his portrait signed "Gilly," which was both intimate and anonymous. For she had reached the stage where she had to tell somebody or die.

The nice man was sympathetic and understanding, and, since his mind was on results rather than causes, he gave her no cause for embarrassment.

Mr. Orsan lived in a beautiful house overlooking Hyde Park, but on its unfashionable frontier. His connection with his business was a very slight one. For two hours a day he attended his head office and dictated reproofs to the various heads of departments, watched salary lists with the eye of an eagle, punished the petty defalcations which are the common experience of storekeepers, told his general manager the story of how he started life with nothing and by his industry and application to business had amassed a fortune—and then went back to his room, the windows of which looked across the budding green of trees, and composed the letter or the lecture (for he was in demand as a speaker at literary societies) which occupied his attention at the moment.

This writing-room was a lovely saloon, all gold and jade green, with a great marble fireplace, and it was furnished in Empire style. It was very unlike the cupboards where his shop assistants slept, and bore no comparison with the hovels in which his tenants lived and died.

Mr. Orsan was strong for gentility, and the footman who took a card to him wore knee breeches, with the golden tassels of aiguillettes dangling from his shoulders. Mr. Orsan read the card, fingered his greying side whiskers, rubbed his bristling black eyebrows, and pursed his lips.

"Superintendent Bliss? Who the deuce is Superintendent Bliss? Show him in, Thomas."

Bliss entered and instantly annoyed the great man by expressing, by his attitude and manner, less deference and respect to him than he felt was due from a public servant. Bliss put his hat on the floor and sat down uninvited

—an objectionable action to Mr. Orsan, who was strong for proper behaviour.

"Well, sir," he said impatiently, "I presume you wish to see me about that defaulting cashier of mine? I would much rather you saw my general manager. I do not, as a rule—"

"I haven't come to discuss defaulting cashiers, Mr. Orsan," said Bliss brusquely. "My visit is in regard to a letter you wrote which was published in this morning's *Megaphone* dealing with the criminal classes and the urgent need for extending capital punishment for felonies."

* * * *

Mr. Orsan sat back in his chair, put the tips of his fingers together, and inclined his head more graciously. That Scotland Yard should take notice of his views on criminals was especially flattering.

"Of course, of course! I had forgotten that," he said. "I think you will agree with me, inspector—or superintendent, or whatever you are—that the only way to deal with the habitual criminal—"

"I'm not even asking you for your views on the habitual criminal," said Bliss, who had no finesse.

Mr. Orsan hated being interrupted, and showed it.

"In your reference to criminals," Bliss went on, unconscious of the fact that he had ruffled the magnate, "you spoke of a certain man, The Ringer. You said it was disgraceful that the police allowed this criminal to remain at large and that his crimes had gone unpunished."

"And I hold to that opinion," said Mr. Orsan firmly. "I suppose it has rubbed you up the wrong way at Scotland Yard? Well, I'm afraid I can't help that. As a public man, writing on a matter of national interest, I must speak the views which, as I feel, are generally held."

Bliss laughed.

"It is very interesting to read your views, Mr. Orsan, but we aren't very much troubled by them. Scotland Yard is there to be kicked, and if we weren't kicked we should think something unusual was happening. I merely came to warn you that it is a very dangerous thing to mention this man or to draw attention to yourself in the way you have, especially in view of the fact that we have reason to believe he has been staying at Hythe recently."

Mr. Orsan frowned. Hythe? It had a familiar sound.

"Why at Hythe?" he asked.

"There is a young lady at Hythe who calls herself Mrs. Tredmayne, but is, I believe, a girl named Brown who was recently in your employ. I don't know whether she has any grievance against you; I only know that to all appearances she has reasonable grounds for grievance. She was once your secretary-housekeeper—rather a pretty girl—"

"I know all about Miss Brown," snapped Orsan. "A very nice—er—young lady who had the misfortune to…Well, I don't wish to discuss it with you, and—"

"It is unnecessary to discuss it at all, Mr. Orsan," said Bliss in his hard, metallic voice. "It would take more than Miss Brown to shock Scotland Yard. The only point is that if the man who was living in the same boarding-house at Hythe was The Ringer, then there is every reason for you to expect trouble. I think it is very undesirable that you should call attention to yourself and your antagonism to The Ringer."

Mr. Orsan rose and towered over the detective.

"Let me tell you, Mr. Bliss, that I am surprised to hear you offer such a suggestion! Is it not my duty as a citizen to denounce this man—aye, and to denounce the police for their laxity in their treatment of him?

"So far from avoiding any reference to The Ringer, I shall make it the subject of my next letter to the *Megaphone*—the editor of which is a great personal friend of mine," he added significantly, as though that statement conveyed a terrifying threat.

Bliss shrugged his shoulders and rose, picking up his hat.

"Does it occur to you that it would be a simple matter to use you as a bait to catch this man?" he asked. "Or that it might make our task considerably easier if we encouraged you to denounce, as you call it, The Ringer?"

* * * *

That had not occurred to Mr. Orsan; it did not occur to him now. After Thomas had shown the visitor from the premises Mr. Orsan pushed aside the sheet on which he had been inscribing his remedies for poverty (remedies which did not include decent housing and higher wages) and, ringing for his secretary, gave orders that every available piece of data concerning Henry Arthur Milton, better known as The Ringer, should be accumulated for reference. Having done this he began a letter to the editor of the *Megaphone*, which began:

Sir,—

When Pliny the Younger spoke of that "indolent but agreeable condition of doing nothing," he surely had in view the attitude of the police towards "the biggest rascal that ever walked on two legs" (see Pliny's letters)—The Ringer….

He wrote with vehemence, with passion, with a tremendous sense of importance. He called for an instant investigation of police methods, he hinted that Scotland Yard was not sacrosanct, and introduced such Latin tags as

Non sibi sed patriœ, to justify his own energy, and *Quis custodiet ipsos custodes*, to explain the inaction of the police.

His letter did not create a furore: little bits of it were cut out by the gentleman who "made up" the *Megaphone* in order to allow space for a dog-racing advertisement; but it certainly attracted attention. At Scotland Yard Bliss read the letter and grinned mirthlessly.

"It is a pity," he said, "that the old man forgot that 'Those whom the gods destroy write letters to the newspapers.'"

Inspector Mander smiled his disapproval of the flippancy.

"There's a lot in what he says," he stated.

Mr. Bliss turned cold eyes upon his incompetent assistant.

"There's a lot in what you say, and yet you're hardly worth listening to," he said unkindly.

Two days after the epistle was published the inevitable letter came to Mr. Orsan. It was typewritten, posted in the north-west district of London, and began without conventional introduction.

"You're a very amusing letter-writer. Are you as good a debater? I am thinking of giving a Christmas dinner to all your unfortunate tenants, and I have taken the Herbert Hall for that purpose. At nine o'clock in the evening I am prepared to appear on the platform and debate with you the question of Capital Punishment. Show this to Bliss. Reply through the advertisement columns of the 'Megaphone.'"

It was signed, in a flourishing hand, "Henry Arthur Milton."

"Swank," said Mr. Orsan vulgarly.

He telephoned through to Scotland Yard, and was infuriated when Bliss, with the greatest coolness, invited him to call on him.

"I shall be at home all the afternoon," repeated Mr. Orsan.

"So shall I," was the reply. "Call at three o'clock. I may be able to give you exactly ten minutes."

Swallowing his pride, the magnate drove down in his limousine to Scotland Yard and suffered the indignity of being kept waiting for a quarter of an hour before he was admitted to the bare businesslike office where Superintendent Bliss worked.

The detective took the letter and read it through.

"Well?" he asked, when he had finished. "Are you going to take up the challenge?"

"Take up the challenge?" Mr. Orsan stared at him. "Do you seriously suggest that this man will come to the Herbert Hall to debate...it's preposterous!"

"If he says he'll come to the Herbert Hall, he'll come," said Bliss. "Exactly what will happen to you I don't know, but I should imagine something unpleasant. You'd better put the advertisement in, and I will do my best to keep you from harm."

Mr. Orsan was not frightened; he was merely surprised.

"Do you mean to tell me, inspector—"

"Superintendent," murmured Bliss.

"Does it really matter what you are?" asked Mr. Orsan impatiently. "You're a public servant, which is all that concerns me. Do you really mean to tell me that you take this balderdash seriously?"

"I certainly do, and I advise you to do the same."

* * * *

In the course of the next few days Mr. Orsan attained to the eminence of a public figure. Another letter from him, which quoted that received from The Ringer, was published in every newspaper in the land.

It was ascertained that the Herbert Hall, which is one of the largest in London and is situated in South Kensington, had been engaged through an agent for the use of an unknown patron, who had paid the rent in advance; and that a large firm of caterers had received orders to provide refreshments for three thousand people. They also had been paid in cash.

There was some suggestion that the proprietors of the hall should cancel the letting, in the public interest, but Scotland Yard got busy to prevent this. Mander interviewed the owners of the hall and the caterers and told them to let matters stand as they were.

He himself was, at his own request, put in charge of the police arrangements.

"I want this chance, chief, to wipe out the mistake I made over the Lumière case," he pleaded. "I shall make no mistake here."

Bliss was unwilling to do this, but Mander's appeal was seconded by a high authority, for the inspector had made many useful friends, and in the end Bliss yielded.

"It's a chance for you, Mander, but it's very nearly your last chance," he said. "I hate putting you in charge, and I doubt if I'd do it if I wasn't convinced that whoever tackles The Ringer at this little Christmas party of his will get it in the neck."

Mander smiled.

"If he's a man of his word he'll have to be a magician to get away."

"He's a man of his word, all right. Take the case, and God help you."

It was not difficult to secure guests at this party. Mr Orsan's tenants lived in solid blocks, in little mean streets where every house looked like the other, in tenements which had been up to date in the 'seventies and were no longer up to date. To every occupier came an invitation, printed on a private press. Mr. Orsan became famous. He was pointed out in restaurants as the man who would meet The Ringer in debate.

Superintendent Bliss had made only one suggestion to his subordinate.

"I advise you to have four doctors within reach of the platform and an ambulance ready to rush Orsan to the hospital," he said.

"Why four?" asked Mander.

"Two for each of you," snarled Bliss, and again Mr. Mander smiled.

"If he turns up I'm a Dutchman."

"You are what you are and nothing can alter you," said Bliss bitterly.

It was on Christmas Eve that Mr. Orsan received the second letter.

"Do not fail me. If you do not turn up I shall wait for you on the platform for ten minutes, and no longer."

But, for the moment, Mr. Orsan was not concerned about The Ringer. A new protagonist had appeared in the field. He had received a communication from a Mr. Arthur Agnis, and not only a communication, but a call.

Mr. Agnis, a shock-headed, bearded man, was a strenuous opponent of capital punishment. He had, he said, argued against capital punishment wherever the English language was spoken, and he came with the request that if The Ringer did not turn up he might be allowed to argue in his stead. He seemed a respectable man, was well dressed, and treated Mr. Orsan with the greatest deference. Moreover, he arrived in his own car.

"My point is this, sir," he said. "You're being taken down to the Herbert Hall, and it is pretty certain that The Ringer will not appear—it's a hoax, if ever there was one. Why not let us have the debate?"

It seemed a very good idea, especially as Mr. Orsan had his speech already in type.

As a matter of precaution, he communicated with Scotland Yard.

"Arthur Agnis!" said Mander softly. "By gad!"

He got on the telephone to Orsan.

"By all means, let him come," he said. "Where does he live?"

"I didn't trouble to ask him," said Mr. Orsan. "He is telephoning me tonight to get my decision. He seems a very charming and well-spoken man."

"He would be!" said Mander, smiling to himself.

There were certain arrangements to be made. Mounted police were drafted to control the crowd of curious onlookers that surrounded the hall; policemen in plain clothes were called for duty by the thousand, and orders were given that only ticket-holders were to be admitted.

"Don't forget," warned Bliss on Christmas afternoon, when he met his subordinate at the Yard, "that Henry Arthur Milton does not depend upon

69

wigs and beards. When he impersonates a man he *is* that man. His voice, his gestures, his tricks of speech—he has the whole box of tricks."

"Trust me," said Mander.

"I'd rather not," replied Bliss, and left the man to his fate.

The ticket-holders began to queue up as early as four o'clock in the afternoon. By seven the hall was packed, and the tables which had been set on the floor and in the galleries were filled. A band had been engaged to keep them occupied and amused; there was to be dancing after the debate.

At half-past eight Mander, accompanied by four armed officers, went to Orsan's house and was shown up into his beautiful library-sitting-room. When they went in the urbane gentleman looked up over his glasses and pointed to chairs.

"Sit down, please. I want to finish this letter to the *Megaphone*."

He wrote steadily for a quarter of an hour, then put down his pen, blotted the paper, and, collecting the sheets together, folded them into an envelope.

"It has occurred to me that this man might be—er—a suspicious person."

"That's already occurred to me, sir," said Mr. Mander. "You needn't worry about him. The moment he gives his name at the door he will practically be surrounded by police. We have left a space in front of the platform so that he can come forward, because we want to see just what he is going to do."

"He's not likely to do anything—rash, is he?" asked the other nervously.

"Trust me, sir," said Mander. It was a favourite expression of his—and, happily, the man he guarded did not know the right answer.

* * * *

The car was waiting at the door, and in this the five were driven to the Herbert Hall and admitted at a private entrance. As the hands of Mr. Orsan's watch pointed to nine its wearer walked forward on to the platform with his bodyguard, and the audience, forgetting, in the cheer of the blessed feast, their natural and year-long grievance against their oppressor, cheered in the sycophantic way of tenants saluting their landlord.

He went nervously to the platform and stood with folded hands, waiting. There was a deathly hush; privileged reporters who had been admitted made a brief examination of the hall, wondering whence The Ringer would come.

Then there was a stir; a bearded man strode into the beam of the lime-light, which was focused, by Mander's orders, not on the figure standing on the stage, but upon the space where the debater would take his position.

"As The Ringer hasn't come," he began, in a high-pitched voice, "I'd like to take issue with you, Mr. Orsan, on the subject of capital punishment.

I've got a few notes here—"

He reached for his hip pocket. Before he could withdraw its contents a cloud of detectives surrounded him. Before anybody in the hall realised what was happening he was whisked away.

"I think that's all, sir," smiled Mander. "I shouldn't advise you to stay any longer; we don't want to take any unnecessary chances."

He left to the bodyguard the task of escorting the charge to safety, and dashed off to interrogate his bearded prisoner. Mr. Agnis was livid of face, violent of tongue.

"You pull my beard again," he screamed, "and I'll beat the head off you! All England shall ring with this outrage!"

"It's a real beard," muttered one of the detectives to Mander, "and he's got papers on him that prove he's what he says he is."

The inspector examined these quickly. A horrible mistake had been made.

"Why did you come here at all?" he asked.

"Because I was invited here," howled Agnis. "I was brought down from Manchester. A gentleman gave me twenty-five pounds to come and debate the question of capital punishment with old Orsan."

The eyes of Mander and his second-in-command met blankly.

"Anyway," said Mander after a while, "that disposes of The Ringer. I said he'd never come, and he hasn't. Now, if anybody looks silly over this business it's Bliss."

He went back to Scotland Yard and found Bliss waiting impatiently for news.

"Why the hell didn't you telephone?" said the superintendent savagely when he told the story.

He was out of Scotland Yard, flying to Mr. Orsan's house, before Mander could think of an adequate reply.

One of the resplendent footmen admitted him.

"Yes, sir, Mr. Orsan is at home; he's been home some time."

"Where is he?"

"In his writing-room, sir."

But Orsan was not in his writing-room. He was not in his bedroom. Eventually they found him trussed up in a small box-room at the top of the house, gagged and handcuffed, and there he had been since three o'clock that afternoon, when The Ringer went for him through a private passage leading from the garage, before he made himself up at his leisure in Mr. Orsan's own bedroom, wearing Mr. Orsan's own clothes (even Mr. Orsan's own watch), and had appeared on the platform at the Herbert Hall.

He had not gone alone. The library safe had been forced; some seven thousand pounds' worth of negotiable securities had been taken. How negotiable they were Miss Brown could have told them, for a month after the robbery she received bank-notes to their full value, with a line of writing which ran:

"A present from Horace."

Which was curious, because she knew nobody named "Horace."

Chapter 8

The End of Mr. Bash—the Brutal

"Bash" was really clever. He stood out from all other criminals in this respect. For the ranks of wrongdoers are made up of mental deficients—stupid men who invent nothing but lies. They are what the brilliant Mr. Coe calls in American criminals "jail bugs." The English criminal, because he does not dope, becomes a pitiable and whining creature who demands charity, and the American criminal develops into a potential homicide.

Bash was a constant, but not, in the eyes of the law, an habitual criminal. He had never been charged because he had never been caught. He was an expert safe-breaker and worked alone.

He might have been forgiven, and, indeed, admired by scientific and disinterested students of criminology for his burglaries, for he had none of the nasty habits of part-time burglars, which means that he was never in the blue funk that they were. But Bash earned his name of infamy from a practice which neither police nor public ever forgave. He was never content to work with the knowledge that there was a watchman sleeping peaceably on the premises he was supposed to guard.

He would first seek out the unfortunate man, and, with a short and flexible life-preserver, beat him to insensibility. The same happened to several unhappy servants. He spared neither man nor woman. He had been suspected of doing worse than bludgeon, but no complaint had been made public.

It was Inspector Mander who suggested that Bash was a name by which one Henry Arthur Milton might be identified. He developed his thesis with great skill but little logic, and Mr. Bliss, on whom the interesting theories were tried, listened with a face that betrayed none of the emotions he felt.

"He has got the same methods as The Ringer; in many ways he has the same identity—nobody knows him—"

"He may be Count Pujoski," suggested Bliss.

"Who is he?" asked Mander, interested.

"I don't know—nobody knows. There isn't such a person," said Bliss calmly. "If the fact that you don't know two people proves that you know one means anything, how much easier it is not to know three!"

73

Mander pondered this, having no sense of humour.

"I don't see how—" he began.

"Get on with your funny story," said Bliss.

But Mr. Mander had run short of arguments.

"I often wonder why you don't write a pantomime" (Bliss could be foully offensive) "or a children's play! The Ringer! Good God!"

All his contempt was comprehended in that pious ejaculation.

"The only connection I see," said Bliss, "is the possible connection between The Ringer and our bashing friend. The newspapers have got hold of the story of what happened to Colonel Milden's parlourmaid, and that is the sort of thing that will make The Ringer see red. If he isn't too busy putting the world right in other directions and he gives his mind to Mr. Bash, we shall be saved a lot of trouble."

Bliss had discovered by painful experience that The Ringer had extraordinary sources of information; it was pretty certain that he was, in some rôle or other, in the closest touch with the great underworld of London. It was equally certain that none of the men he employed had the least idea of his identity.

There was a reward offered for his capture, and the average criminal would sell his own brother at a price—especially if he were certain that no kick was coming from the associates of the man betrayed.

Who was Bash? At least a dozen men in London must know—the receivers who fenced his stolen property, close confidants who had at some time or other worked with him. But these would never tell.

There were times when Superintendent Bliss sighed for the good old days of the rack and the thumb-screw. What they would not squeak to the police, however, they might very well tell to a "sure-man."

* * * *

In Penbury Road, Hampstead, was a small detached house with a tiny garden forecourt and a narrow strip of garden behind. Here dwelt Mr. Sanford Hickler, a man of thirty-five, athletic, sandy-haired, slightly bald. He was both arty and crafty, and his house in Hampstead was full of arty and crafty objects—ancient dower chests that might have dated back to the Middle Ages and certainly came from the Midlands.

Mr. Hickler had greeny wallpaper and yellowy candlesticks, and his study was littered with junk that he called "pieces." Some of these pieces he had picked up in Italy, and some he had picked up in Greece; most of them would hardly be picked up at all. And there were a few maternity homes for the *lepidoptera* family hanging on the wall, which were distinguished by the name of tapestry.

Mr. Hickler's hobby was literature. He was a graduate of a famous university, and he knew literature to be something that was no longer manufactured. He studied literature as one studies a dead language or the ruins of Ur. It did not belong to today. With the passing of the years his mind had broadened. He had come to the place where the works of the late Mr. Anthony Trollope were literature.

He was sitting one evening reading the sonnets of Shakespeare when there was a knock at the door, and his maid, who was also his cook, came in. She had just put on the brown uniform and the coffee-coloured cap and apron which were the visible evidence of her transition.

"A Mrs. Something or other to see you, sir. She came in a car."

Mr. Hickler put down his sonnets.

"Mrs. Something or other came in a car? What does she want?"

"I don't know, sir—she said it's about books."

"Show her into the drawing-room," he said.

A great many boring people went to see Mr. Hickler about books. He had a local reputation as a poetaster.

"Very good."

He put a slip of paper to mark his place in the volume he had been reading, and went up the short, narrow passage to the tiny room, more arty and crafty than any of the others, since it was furnished with one settle, a spinet, two Medici prints, and a rush carpet. And there he saw a figure that was out of all harmony with the æsthetic surroundings.

The lady was big, squat, and old-fashioned; a more revolting figure he never hoped to see. Her hair was obviously dyed; a large and fashionable hat sat at a large and unfashionable angle over her spurious locks. Her face was powdered a dead white, and she exhaled a perfume that made Mr. Hickler shudder.

The modishness of her headgear was discounted somewhat by the length of her skirt and the antiquity of her fur coat.

"No, thank you, I won't sit down," she said in a shrill voice. "You're Mr. Hickler? Will you see this for me, please?"

He took the book she offered to him in her large, gloved hand, and saw at a glance that it was a veritable treasure—the very rare Commentaries of Messer Aglapino, the Venetian. Turning the leaves reverently, he peered down at the print, for the lights in his house were so shaded that it hardly seemed worth while to have lights at all.

"Yes, madam, this is a very rare book—probably worth three or four hundred pounds. I envy you your possession."

He handed the book back with a courteous little bow.

"Mrs.—?"

"Mrs. Hubert Verity. You probably know our family. They are Shropshire people. I only wish my nephew was Shropshire in spirit as well as in birth."

She raised her black eyebrows and closed her eyes. Evidently her nephew was not especially popular.

"Won't you sit down?" he asked.

She shook her head.

"I prefer to stand."

Her high-pitched voice was very painful to the sensitive ears of Mr. Hickler.

"I don't know why I should trouble you with my affairs; but I never could stand a miser, and Gordon is a miser. My dear husband was thoroughly deceived by him or he would never have left him thirty thousand pounds, which was quite as much as, if not more than, he left me.

"I've had a lot of misfortune owing to these terrible Stock Exchange people who tell you shares are going up when they're really going down—and well they know it! And when I went to my nephew today to ask him for a trifling loan—I must put The Cedars in a state of repair, with dear Alfred coming back from South Africa in the spring—he showed me his passbook!

"I could have laughed if I wasn't so enraged. I said to him: 'My dear boy, do you imagine that I am a fool? Do you think I don't know you well enough to know that you keep your money fluid, like the miser that you are!' It was a dreadful thing to call one's own nephew, but Gordon Stourven deserves every word. I could tell the Income Tax Commissioners a few things about Gordon."

She tossed her grotesque head and simpered meaningly. And then she looked at the book.

"Three hundred pounds…and I want the money very badly. I suppose you wouldn't like to buy it?"

The book was worth five hundred at least, but Mr. Hickler hesitated. His inclination was to buy; his sense of discretion told him to temporise.

"I am not in a position now to buy the book," he said, "but if you would give me the first offer, perhaps I could take your name and address."

She gave the name of her house in Kensington.

"I shall be out of town until next Wednesday week. I go to Paris for my dresses."

She said this importantly, and Mr. Hickler did not laugh.

"I like you: you're businesslike. If Gordon Stourven had half your straightforwardness life would be ever so much more enjoyable. That man is so mean that he will not have a telephone in his office. I said to him: 'My dear boy, do you imagine I'm coming through this horrible city to Bucklersbury and climb to the top floor of a wretched office building just to see you?' In fact, I offered to pay for the telephone myself...."

* * * *

Mr. Hickler listened, apparently without interest: and later accompanied the lady as she waddled to her car. She insisted upon leaving the book behind, and for this concession he was grateful.

He waited till the car had disappeared and then he went back to the house, closed the door, and took the volume into his sitting-room, turning the pages idly. Somebody had been looking through it that very day: there was a bookmark—a credit slip from the Guaranty Trust, of that day's date, and it showed the exchange of a draft for 180,000 dollars into English currency.

Mr. Hickler turned the slip over and over. The book had been in the possession of Mr. Gordon Stourven; and here was Mr. Gordon Stourven's name scribbled in pencil on the top of the slip. A man who dabbled in cash finance, obviously, and a wealthy man. It was all very interesting, all very foreign to the art and the craft and the æstheticism in which Mr. Hickler lived his normal life.

The next day business took him to the City, and he drove down in the cheap little car that he permitted himself—the car that has its hundred-thousand duplicates up and down the land. There were two blocks of offices in Bucklersbury, but the first he entered was the one he sought.

Mr. Gordon Stourven's name was painted in black on one of the many opalescent slides that filled an indicator. He lived on the fifth floor and his number was 979. Mr. Hickler took the elevator, toiled down the long corridor, and after a while stopped before a door on the glass panel of which was "Gordon Stourven," and, in smaller characters at the bottom left-hand corner:

> *The Vaal Heights Gold Mining Syndicate.*
> *The Leefontein Deeps.*
> *United American Finance Syndicate.*

Since the panel also announced that this was the general office, he turned the handle and stepped in.

An L-shaped counter formed a sort of lobby, in which he waited until his tapping on its surface brought a bespectacled and unprepossessing young lady.

"Mr. Stourven's out," she said promptly and hoarsely. "He's gone to lunch with his aunt."

Mr. Hickler smiled faintly.

"I had better wait and see him," he said, and held up a little parcel. "This book is the property of the lady and I wish to return it."

She looked at him for a long time before she decided to lift the flap of the counter and invite him across the linoleum-covered floor to a small inner office. She pulled a chair from the wall.

"You'd better sit down," she said jerkily. "I don't know whether I'm doing right—I've only been at this place for two days. The young lady before me got sacked for pinching—I mean stealing—I mean taking a penny-halfpenny stamp. You wouldn't think anybody would be so mean, would you? But she was—he told me himself! And he's worth thousands. I'm going myself today."

"I'm sorry to hear that," smiled Mr. Hickler.

"I'm only staying to oblige him," explained the bespectacled girl. "He mislaid his keys this morning and the way he went on to me about it was a positive disgrace. Why should I pinch anything out of his old safe?"

* * * *

Hickler did not encourage conversation. He very badly wished to be alone. Presently his desire was gratified.

There was the safe, embedded in the wall. Curious, he mused, what faith even intelligent people have in five sides of masonry! It was an American safe that grew unfashionable, except among the burglaring classes, twenty years before. He examined it thoughtfully. Two holes drilled, one below and one above the lock…even that wasn't necessary. A three-way key adjustment would open that in a quarter of an hour.

He stepped to the door softly and looked through a glass-panelled circle in the opaque glass. The girl was at her desk, writing laboriously, her mouth moving up and down with every figure she wrote. He put his hand in his hip pocket and took out his little cosh—a leather-plaited life-preserver.

The girl could be dealt with very expeditiously; but the danger was too great. Stourven might return at any moment. He took another and a closer scrutiny of the safe and smiled. Then he went to the desk and examined the memoranda and the papers.

The only thing that really interested him was the carbon sheet of a typewritten letter—and a letter so badly typewritten that he guessed it was the work of the disgruntled young lady with spectacles. It was addressed to a Broad Street Trust Company and bore that day's date.

Dear Mr. Lein,—

I am prepared to close the deal tomorrow and will meet you at your lawyer's as arranged. I do not agree with you that I have a great bargain. The property must be developed—it seems to have fallen into a pretty bad state of disrepair.

In the circumstances I do not think that £18,700 is a very attractive price. However, I never go back on my word. I quite understand that lawyers require cash payments, and in any circumstances my cheque wouldn't be of much use to you, for I keep a very small balance at the bank.

Mr. Hickler replaced the letter carefully where he had found it. He had not removed his gloves since he left his house. It was a peculiarity of Mr. Hickler that he never removed his gloves except in his own home. People thought it was because he had been nicely brought up, but that was not the reason.

He went into the outer office, still carrying the book.

"By the way, I don't think you should have invited me into Mr. Stourven's private office. If I were you, I shouldn't say you took me there." He smiled benignantly at her.

Yes, he was glad he didn't have to tackle this bespectacled imbecile. She looked like one of those thin-skulled people with whom one might easily have an accident; and she was wiry and vital—the sort of shrimp who, if one didn't get her at the first crack, would scream and raise hell.

On his way downstairs he stopped to inquire at the janitor's office whether there were any offices to let and what were the services. The janitor told him.

"By the way, what time do the cleaners start their operations?" he asked.

This was rather an important matter. The hours the office cleaners arrived and left very often determined an operation.

They came on at midnight, explained the porter. So many of the offices were let to stockbrokers, who in the busy season worked very late. There were two entrances to the building; the other was an automatic lift, which tenants could operate themselves, the general elevator going out of action at 9 p.m.

All this Mr. Hickler learned, and more. There were two offices to let in the basement. The porter very kindly took him down and flattered them to their face.

"No, sir, I go off at six, but we've got a night man on duty. We have to do that because we've a great deal of property and money in this building. One of our tenants, Mr. Stourven, was asking me that very question this morning. He's only been here a fortnight himself—he came from somewhere down in Moorgate. A very nervous gentleman he is too." The porter smiled at the recollection.

Mr. Hickler, who was paying the closest attention to the accommodation of the offices, explained that he thought of founding a small literary society in the City for clerks who, in the hours so crudely devoted to the mastication of beef-steak pudding, might enrich their souls with an acquaintance with the *soufflés* of Keats.

The porter thought it was a very good idea. He did not know who Keats was, but had a dim notion that he was the gentleman who had found a method of destroying beetles and other noxious friends of the pestologist.

* * * *

The little car went back to Hampstead at a slow rate, was garaged in the tiny shed at the end of the garden before Mr. Hickler went into his house, stripped his gloves and gave his mind to the evening's occupation.

He was clever, very clever, because he devoted thought to his trade. He applied to a "transaction" such as tonight's the same minute care, the same thought, the same close analysis as he gave to a disputed and obscure line of one of the earlier English poets.

Nobody knew very much about him; nobody guessed why he had called his tiny cottage "The Plume of Feathers." Even the bronze ornament above the knocker on his door, representing, as it did, such a feathery plume, did not explain his eccentricity.

Yet the name of his house was one of the most careless mistakes he ever committed, and if there had been the remotest suspicion attached to him, if Scotland Yard had been even aware of his existence, the Plume of Feathers would have been illuminating—for it is the name of an inn immediately facing Dartmoor Prison, an inn towards which Mr. Hickler had often cast wistful eyes on his way to the prison fields.

He was not Mr. Hickler then; he was just plain James Connor, doing seven years' penal servitude for robbery with assault, to which sentence had been added a flogging, which he never forgot.

He was prison librarian for some time; cultivated his fine taste in *belles lettres* with the grey-backed volumes of the prison library. Only two men in London knew of his connection with that dreadful period of inaction. One of them, as Bliss rightly surmised, was the greatest of the fences—great because he had never betrayed a client and had never been arrested by the police.

Mr. Hickler expected a telephone call concerning the book, but it did not come. At half-past seven he put a small suitcase and a rough, heavy overcoat in the back of his car, and drove by way of Holloway to the Epping Forest road. Here, in seclusion, he made a rapid change of clothes; drove back to Whitechapel, where he garaged the car, and made his way to Bucklersbury on foot.

The only evidence that the activity of the human hive was slackening was discoverable in the fact that one of the two doors which closed each entrance was already shut. He awaited his opportunity, stepped briskly into the deserted passage, found the automatic lift, and went up to the top floor. The corridor here was, except for one lamp, in darkness. There was no light in any of the offices, and that was a great relief.

Mr. Stourven's outer door was, of course, locked, but only for about three minutes. By that time Mr. Hickler was inside and had shot the bolt. He did not attempt to put on the lights, preferring the use of his own hand-lamp.

Both the outer office and the inner office were empty. He made a quick examination of the cupboards, tried the windows—he was free from all possibility of interruption.

Setting his lamp on the floor, he took the remainder of his tools from his pocket and set to work on the safe—the easiest thing he had ever attempted. In twenty-five minutes the key he had inserted some thirty times gripped the wards of the lock. It went back with a snap. He turned the brass handle and pulled open the heavy door of the safe.

He was on his knees, peering into the interior. He had scarcely time to realise that the safe was empty except for thousands of fragments of thin glass before he fell forward, striking his head on the edge of the safe.

* * * *

Bliss had a letter. It was delivered by a district messenger, and he knew it was from The Ringer before he opened it. It came to him at his private residence.

You will find our friend Bash in office No. 979, Greek House, Bucklersbury. He is, I should imagine, quite dead, so he will not be able to tell you how splendid an actor I am. I went to see him at his artistic little place in Hampstead—my most difficult feat, for I had to keep my knees bent all the time I was talking to him in order to simu-late dumpiness. You should try that some time.

I persuaded him to burgle a safe in my office. Inside the safe I smashed, just before I closed the door, a large tube of the deadliest gas known to science. I will call it X.3 and you will probably know what it is. It was then in liquid form, but, of course, volatilised imme-diately to a terrific volume.

And the moment he opened the door he was dead, I should imag-ine, but you might make sure. And you had better take a gas mask. You are too good a man to lose.

There was no signature but a postscript.

Or why not send Mander without a gas mask?

81

Chapter 9

The Complete Vampire

There was a skid on the road out of St. Mary Church which, since it came before no court and involved no drawing of plans for the further bewilderment of a dazed jury, need not be described in too great detail.

It is sufficient to say that motorcar A took a hairpin turn at thirty-five miles an hour, saw motorcar B proceeding in the opposite direction at about the same pace, and swerved to avoid a collision, both cars being on the wrong side of the road, but A being more on the wrong side than B.

Dropping all alphabetical anonymity, the Hon. Mr. Bayford St. Main's car kept its balance and suffered no harm, but the other waltzed round in its own length, turned turtle into an over-flooded ditch, and its one occupant would most certainly have been drowned if Bay had not had the wit and the muscle to effect a rescue. His strength was as the strength of ten, not because his heart was pure, but because he was terribly exhilarated over his engagement, and even more exhilarated as a result of a lunch he had had with his rather parsimonious father at Torquay.

"Go easy with that Napoleon brandy, my boy! That cost me a hundred and eighty shillings a bottle—and I only got it as a special favour from a *maître d'hôtel* at Monte Carlo."

"Everybody does," said Bay.

Straddling the ditch, he lifted the car sufficiently to allow the imprisoned man to escape.

"Dreadfully sorry—I don't know whose fault it was," said Bay with great politeness. The victim smiled weakly.

"Lots of people have predicted various ends for me," he said, "but nobody suggested that I should die in a ditch."

He was—he announced this with rather ridiculous pomposity—Marksen, the explorer.

"Good Lord!" said Bay, in tones of awe.

He had never heard of Marksen the explorer, but he knew exactly the tone that the moist man expected.

"I'd better take you back to Babbacombe in my car," he began, but at this point the gardener came on the scene. He and his mistress had witnessed the accident from the crest of the high bank which was in the main the real cause of the accident.

"If you'll come up to the house, sir, madam will telephone to Babbacombe to a garage and you'll be able to dry yourself."

Mr. Marksen agreed gratefully, but the tall young man who had overturned him insisted upon returning to the nearest point of civilisation to obtain the necessary breakdown gang. They shook hands soberly at the foot of the stone steps which led from the roadway to madam's invisible demesne.

"I hate to say the trite thing, but you've saved my life—undoubtedly," said Mr. Marksen, whose dignity nothing could ruffle. "To think of the perils I have endured, the dangers I have passed, and then to find myself in a Devonshire ditch...."

"Yes, yes; deuced awkward," replied Bay hastily. He had a wholesome dread of scenes.

"Some day I shall be able to repay you, Mr. St. Main," said Marksen.

He followed the gardener into beautifully-ordered grounds. There were close-cropped lawns and flower beds ablaze with the joyous banners of spring, and a red-roofed little house, just as picturesque as a modern house can be when it is masquerading as an old house. Here was a very stately lady of sixty who wore silk mittens, a white cap, and on the bosom of her black alpaca dress, a large ornament which was cameo on the one side and a hand-painted photograph on the other.

It was a beautifully furnished little house, and when Mr. Marksen had enjoyed a hot bath and had attired himself in the brand-new suit of the gardener (rashly purchased for the funeral of an aunt who took a turn for the better the day the clothes were delivered), Mrs. Reville Ross (this was the name of his hostess) conducted him from room to room, exhibiting her treasures with immodest pride.

There were certain incongruous features which Mr. Marksen could not fail to observe. A cheap crayon enlargement of a cheaper kind of photograph seemed out of place in the sunny drawing-room.

"My dear husband," said Mrs. Ross proudly. "He was killed on the railway but was insured. My daughter." She turned the big cameo to reveal the highly coloured portrait of a pretty girl of sixteen. "You must have heard of her." She mentioned the name of a famous American cinema star. "English!" said Mrs. Ross in triumph. "Everybody thinks she's American. She'd lose her job if it was known she was Betty Ross. I've got a piece of newspaper somewhere—American newspaper—where she says she's never been to England. She comes over secretly every year to stay with me for a month. She worships me, that girl. She bought this house—I got my own servant, shoofer, gardener, car—everything. Nothing's too good for me."

Mr. Marksen listened and was interested. He had been interested ever since he had heard the old lady speak in the good old English of Limehouse and realised that the chatelaine of the pseudo-Elizabethan house was not all that she appeared to be.

Coincidences belong to real life rather than to fiction, and there are three coincidences in this story—one of which does not count; the gardener's name was Fate—Herbert Arthur Fate.

Superintendent Bliss, of Scotland Yard, might have fashioned a poem on this odd fact.

* * * *

Nobody would suspect Mr. Bliss of poetical leanings, yet in truth he was, if not a student, a lover of the more robust forms of poetry.

He invariably referred to Louise Makala as "the lady called Lou," and on two occasions had spoken with her for the good of her soul. Louise was not easily impressed, less readily scared: Superintendent Bliss certainly did not frighten her—she regarded him as a bore, thought once that he was on the sentimental side, and attacked him on that flank, only to discover that what she had thought was mush was really a rigid sense of decency.

Lou had a flat in Grosvenor Street, a magnificent apartment with an impressive approach. She had a butler and a couple of footmen; a night and a day chauffeur; a cottage in the country which bore the same resemblance to a cottage as a hunting-box bears to a tin of sardines; a flat in the Etoile, and a small house in Leicestershire where she kept half a dozen hunters. She was the most beautiful creature that Bliss and the majority of men had ever seen—to have seen her was the principal experience of any man's day, and her occupation in life, reducible to modern terms, was vampire. Her victims were many and they were all immensely rich. She did not select them: they did their own selection.

"Who is that lady?" asked the Honourable George Cestein of the hotel porter at Felles Hotel.

The hotel porter told him she was Miss Blenhardt, that her father was a very rich Australian, and that she had, at the moment, the best suite at the hotel.

The Honourable George followed her from the hotel and picked up the glove, handkerchief, or whatever it was she dropped, and within twenty-four hours....

"Either you sign a cheque for twenty thousand pounds or I will scream and send for the police."

George had no more than kissed her, but why, oh why, had he chosen his own private suite at the Margravine Hotel for this attention?

84

He stared at her horrified. Her dress was torn, her hair dishevelled—but these artistic touches were her very own handiwork. George raved but made a quick decision. Louise's own maid put in an appearance. The open cheque was signed and cashed, George threatening to go immediately to Scotland Yard. She had heard such threats before, would hear them again. The substantial fact was a roll of notes valued at £20,000.

* * * *

The first time she met Bliss she had a moment of panic, but it did not last very long.

"Do you know Sir Roland Perfenn?" he asked her sternly.

And she laughed. For Sir Roland is a Privy Councillor and a great ecclesiastical lawyer, and he was the last person in the world to bear evidence of his very heavy loss.

"Does he say I do?" she asked coolly, and of course Bliss would have to say "No" to that.

"It has come to my notice…" he began, and told the story of the all-too-gallant Sir Roland.

"Produce your Sir Roland, my dear Mr. Bliss," she said. "It is a fairly simple matter—if I remember rightly, his name is in the Telephone Directory."

But Bliss was not in a position to accept her advice. He could, however, talk to her like a father.

"So far you've only caught men who dare not squeal and who would rather pay than look foolish. But sooner or later you'll catch a man who looks like a gentleman and talks like one—but isn't! And you'll go to the Old Bailey, and when the Judge asks what is known about this woman, I shall step up on to the witness stand and say 'This lady is a notorious blackmailer,' and you'll go down for twenty years."

She only laughed.

"When a general loses a battle he's finished," she said, "and if a liontamer makes a mistake he's mauled…and, Mr. Bliss, if you pull that one about the pitcher going often to the well, I'll scream for help! No—if I make a mistake I'll pay. But I shan't make a mistake. Will you have a cocktail?"

Bliss smiled grimly and shook his head.

She was sitting on the arm of a big and expensively covered settee, and she drooped her head on one side and into her fine eyes came a quizzical smile.

"Instead of warning me you ought to ask my help," she said. "I think I'm the only person in London who could catch The Ringer for you!"

Bliss winced at this: he thought the remark a little indelicate in view of The Ringer's more recent success.

"Mind that he does not catch you!" seemed a feeble retort in the circumstances, but she did not gloat over the weakness of his *tu quoque*.

"The Ringer! Good heavens! If Scotland Yard was officered by women he would have been caught years ago! I wish he would try me—look!"

She went to the fireplace and produced something from nowhere—she did not trust him sufficiently to show him the tiny marble-faced door of the wall cupboard.

"Have you a licence for that pistol?" asked Bliss professionally, and she laughed.

"Don't be silly! Of course I have! And I can use it! I really did live in Australia for two years—I was married to an imitation squatter. He had delirium tremens for six months in the year and was recovering the other six. We lived on a lonely station and I was taught gun work by a man who had killed three policemen in the State of Nevada. If I give you The Ringer what do I get—a medal?"

He shook his head.

"It will stand in your favour when you come in front of a Judge," he said.

Lou was very amused.

She made her big mistake six months after this conversation. It was in the matter of "Bay" St. Main—who was young and harum-scarum, and was, as we know, engaged to be married to Rendlesham's youngest and richest daughter. Let us do justice to Bay—when he was invited to a convenient snuggery to take tea with this beautiful chance acquaintance he had no more in his mind than the possibility of a thrilling lark. He had the vanity of a normal young man, which meant that he was vainer than the average woman; and that this lovely creature should so readily succumb to the kind and admiring glances he shot at her was distinctly flattering.

Quite a number of people thought that the tall, fair-haired and classical-featured Bay was immensely wealthy. His father was worth a million, but his father liked to see his money stay home with him. Bayford's allowance was absurdly small—he realised very clearly that the chance of his father's helping him honour a cheque for fifteen thousand pounds was a poor one.

As a matter of fact, he didn't really think at all; he was in that condition of horror and shock which inhibits thought. He could stare, pale-faced, at this lovely being in her self-made dishevelment, and when he did speak his words were ludicrously inadequate.

"Why, you—nasty creature!" he squeaked. "I didn't! I just kissed you. I think you're foul to—to make such a suggestion—I really do!"

Louise had no more regard for youthful horror than for middle-aged vituperation. She stated her terms for the second time.

"Fifteen thousand? I haven't got fifteen thousand pence—"

And then he remembered and gasped. That morning his father-in-law-to-be had placed to his credit exactly that sum. Bay was buying a partnership in an underwriting business—thirty thousand was the purchase price. Pa St. Main's half was to come on the morrow. Bay was to hold a one-third interest of the whole. Louise had very accurate information about the financial standing of her cases.

"Don't talk nonsense," she said. "I know your credit to a penny. You have over sixteen thousand in the Piccadilly branch of the Western Bank."

It was now that Bay St. Main's brain began to function, and he reviewed dismally the possible items of embarrassment. Item No. 1 was St. Main Senior, who already leaned towards devoting his fortune to the establishment of Sailors' Institutes—he had in his early youth served before the mast. Item No. 2 was Lord Rendlesham, a High Churchman who virtuously deplored the laxity of the age. Item No. 3 was Inez Rendlesham, very lovely and austere and intolerant of vulgarity. It was difficult to discover any expression of popular activity, from cross-word puzzles to shingling, that did not come into that category.

And, thinking, Mr. St. Main grew paler and paler.

Eventually he signed the cheque and waited, imprisoned with the enchantress, until the money was drawn. During that time he told her incoherently what he thought of such women as she. Lou, who had heard everything that could be said on the subject much more eloquently put—Sir Ronald had once moved the Court of Arches to tears—listened and did not listen.

She was too bored to tell him just what was her point of view. She could have recited her formulae without thinking. Men are born robbers, unscrupulous, remorseless, pitiless. She stood for avenging womanhood. Men must pay sometimes. Et cetera. What she did say was:

"Yours is a sad case—you might apply to the police or you might find The Ringer and tell him all about it. I'd love to meet him."

Which was very foolish of her.

The time came for the return of the maid and his release. He hurled at her one tremulous malediction, but he did not invent the fiction that he was a close personal friend of the Chief Commissioner. For this she was frankly grateful.

* * * *

Mr. Bayford St. Main went out into the busy street and walked aimlessly, unconsciously westward. To whom should the news be broken? To his father? He closed his eyes and shuddered at the thought. To Rendlesham? Picturing Miss Rendlesham's comments, he had a vision of a broken icicle —irregular and frigid lengths of speech, cold, cutting-edged.

His mind searched frantically for rich relations, for wealthy and philanthropic friends. There was nobody in the wide world to whom he could appeal.

"Why—Mr. St. Main, I declare!"

Bay turned and blinked owlishly at the man who had laid an almost affectionate hand on his arm.

"Hallo…. Mr.—um—eh—Marksen, of course." Bay gripped at the murmured reminder, though who Mr. Marksen was—"Oh, yes, the—um—I hope you weren't fearfully ill after that car business?"

He made an instant appraisement of his companion. Mr. Marksen might be very rich—some of these exploring johnnies are: they find buried cities and unbury them, and dig up all sorts of gold things. Unless, of course, they go exploring the North Pole, when they have to be supported by public subscriptions. He looked rather like that kind in his well-worn golf suit, his foul and massive briar pipe, his gold-rimmed spectacles, and little yellow moustache. He had grown the last since they last met, thought Bay. Here, however, he was wrong. Mr. Marksen had the moustache before the accident, but had lost it in the ditch—and his spectacles.

"I could have sworn I saw you coming out of Lethley Court. I used to have a friend who lived in that hotel, and somebody was telling me the other day that—um—quite a notorious—um—person lived there. A lady called… well, well, well, it is no business of mine."

Bay looked at his companion aghast.

"A—a lady?" he stammered.

"More or less," said Mr. Marksen, "more or less. A friend of mine got into serious trouble over—um—a perfectly innocent folly, and I was able to help him; but you wouldn't be interested—"

Bay was more than interested—he was enthralled.

"Come round to my flat, will you?" he asked urgently.

Mr. Marksen looked at his watch and hesitated before he said "Yes."

* * * *

Remember always that Bliss spoke the truth when he said that The Ringer did not merely dress, but lived the part he played.

His insatiable curiosity had brought him on to the track of the lady called Lou. He had been standing within six feet of the entrance to the Lethley Court Hotel when Lou and her victim had driven up, but, not being quite sure of the method, had missed the maid when she went out to cash the cheque. There was no question at all in his mind when, eventually, Bay had staggered out of the hotel with a face the colour of chalk. Curiously enough, it was only then that he recognised his rescuer. Perhaps Bay's face was that colour after he had fished a brother motorist from beneath an overturned car.

Bay had his apartment near Bury Street, and the man in the golf suit strode by his side, smoking his big pipe furiously, and spoke no word until they were alone in the sitting-room which looks out upon Ryder Street.

"I'm going to tell you something," said Bay with a desperate effort to be philosophical. "I've been fearfully, badly caught—naturally, you'll think I'm a fearful cad and all that sort of thing, but I swear to you that I hadn't any idea of anything—you know what I mean?"

Happily, Mr. Marksen knew what he meant otherwise, from the disjointed narrative which followed, he might have gained only the scrappiest idea of what Mr. Bayford St. Main rightly described as his fearful predicament.

"Fifteen thousand—humph!" said Marksen. "And the money isn't yours? Do you mind if I say 'humph' again? I don't know what it means, but it seems the correct thing to say. Anyway, I will get the money back."

Bay gaped at him.

"How?… when?"

"I'll ask her for it; the cheque will come to you tonight."

Mr. St. Main did not believe him.

"You need not worry about whether the cheque will be honoured or not —it will be," said Mr. Marksen thoughtfully. "The only doubt I have in my mind is whether she has an heroic streak. You wouldn't be able to tell me much about that. If she has that slither of theatrical heroism in her make-up, everything may be deucedly complicated. However…did she say anything when you were rude to her?"

Bay tried to think.

"Yes—she said I might apply to that johnny who is always doing something ghastly—The Ringer, that was the feller! She said she'd love to meet him."

"Dear me," said Mr. Marksen, shocked. "Whatever will she say next?"

He ambled out without a word of farewell. Bay was not in a condition to protest at his abrupt exit.

* * * *

The lady called Lou rarely left her Grosvenor Street flat after dinner. The theatres and the fashionable restaurants knew her not. Invariably she dined at home, sometimes alone, sometimes with one she had marked for treatment. The vanity of men! Seldom did a victim tell his dearest friend of his experience. There was an occasion when she had caught in successive weeks two close friends neither of whom was aware of the other's misfortune.

This night she had dined alone, and had retired to her beautiful little drawing-room to draw cheques and to examine accounts. Her overhead bill was a heavy one. There was the flat and an apartment very occasionally used, but which was sometimes very handy.

She was, by the ordinary tests, a strictly proper lady. Her "cases" might call her blackmailer—they could not truthfully call her worse. She was businesslike, cool-blooded, and a shrewd investor in real estate; never drank, seldom smoked, and certainly never gambled. So methodical was she that when the second footman came into the room and announced that the Marquis de Crevitte-Soligny was waiting in the little sitting-room, she was thrown off her balance, and consulted her engagement book with a puzzled expression.

"The Marquis de Crevitte—? Show him in, Bennett."

He might be a friend of a friend; the visit a consequence of an enthusiastic description.

She did not know the tall, white-haired man with the trim, grey moustache, who bowed over her hand. He was handsome, tall, soldierly, and in the lapel of his faultless evening coat was the red rosette of an *officier*.

"Madame does not remember me?" he asked in French.

She shook her head.

"I ask a thousand pardons, but I do not, Monsieur le Marquis."

"Good!"

This time he spoke in English, turned slowly and, walking to the door, locked it with great deliberation.

In an instant she was at the fireplace, the marble-faced cupboard swung open, but before her hand could close on the butt of the automatic—

"Don't touch that. I am covering you with an ugly little pistol that fires shot—it would not kill you, but it would make such alterations to your face that you would be compelled to go out of business. Turn!"

She turned, empty-handed.

"Who are you?" she asked, and she saw him smile.

"I am the man you expressed a desire to meet—The Ringer!"

She stared at him incredulously.

"The Ringer? That's a wig, is it?"

He nodded.

"Sit down, sister brigand! You caught a young friend of mine today for fifteen thousand pounds."

Not a muscle of her face moved.

"I'm afraid you're talking about something that I do not understand—" she began.

He laughed softly and laid the squat pistol on the table, drew up a chair, and sat down.

"This is going to be a longer business than I thought, Mrs. Rosler."

Now he had got beneath her guard, for he saw her wince.

"I'm not blaming you for preying on naughty-minded men. You deserve all that they lose. You choose them with such care that I can only admire you—"

There was a knock. The Ringer moved silently to the door and as silently turned the key.

"Come in," said Lou breathlessly. Pink spots burnt in her two cheeks— there was a light in her eyes that stood for triumph. It was Bennett, the footman.

"Mr. Bliss, madam."

She looked at The Ringer steadily; he was standing by the table, his hand hiding the pistol.

"Show him up," she said steadily.

Before he could speak the door was opened wider; evidently Bliss was on the landing waiting. He glanced from the girl to the immaculate-looking foreigner.

"I can see you later, Miss Makala—it isn't very important."

"But no," protested The Ringer. "It is I who am *de trop*."

"You can wait where you are." Her voice was hard. She stood now close enough to the half-closed cupboard door to reach for the gun, when Bliss crossed between them.

The Ringer shrugged his shoulders delicately.

"I am in the way, but it does not matter—this gentleman is—?"

"Inspector Bliss, of Scotland Yard!"

The Ringer inclined his head.

"An extraordinary coincidence! You shall advise me, inspector. In Devonshire there is an old lady who lives in a nice house—but she is under the impression that her daughter is Miss Stella Maris, the famous cinema star! And her daughter is no such person! Now should one leave the poor lady in her illusion? Or should one say to her: 'No, madam—your daughter is… whatever she is'?"

Lou's face was whiter than any of her victims had been; the hand that came to her quivering lips shook perceptibly.

"I don't know exactly that I am concerned," said Bliss brusquely; and then to Lou, lowering his voice: "I can get my business over in a minute, Miss Makala. Have you ever met a man named Marksen?"

He described Mr. Marksen even as she was shaking her head.

"We believe it is The Ringer—he has been making inquiries about you, and every description we have had is the same. Do you know any private detective of that name?"

"No," she said.

Bliss turned to scrutinise the other occupant of the room. That gentleman was gazing at himself in a mirror, gently smoothing his moustache.

"Who is this gentleman?" he asked.

She cleared her voice.

"The Marquis de Crevitte-Soligny," she said in a low tone. "I have known him for years."

Bliss stayed only long enough to give her instructions as to what she must do if Mr. Marksen called. She listened with apparent absorption.

They heard the street door close on the detective.

"Now," said The Ringer cheerfully, "I want you to draw a cheque for fifteen thousand pounds payable to Bayford St. Main."

"And if I don't—?" she challenged.

He smiled in her face.

"I shall go and tell your mother what a naughty girl you are," he said softly, "and that her darling daughter, so far from being a rich cinema star, is a low little vamp—and that, I think, would hurt her more than the death of her dear husband."

He was watching for the effect of this piece of mimicry and saw her face go livid and the fires of hell come into her eyes.

"Don't insult my dear mother!" she breathed.

And then he knew that he had won—he had discovered where the blackmailer could be blackmailed.

* * * *

"Lou's gone out of business," reported Bliss. "She's sold up her flats and gone to live in Devonshire somewhere. I'll bet The Ringer scared her!"

He had: but not in the way Mr. Bliss thought.

Chapter 10

The Swiss Head Waiter

There was a broad streak of altruism in the composition of Henry Arthur Milton, whose other name was The Ringer. There was, perhaps, as big a streak of sheer impishness. At Scotland Yard they banked on his vanity as being the most likely cause to bring him to ruin, and they pointed out how often he had shown his instant readiness to resent some slight to himself. But Inspector Bliss, who had made a study of the man, could not be prevailed upon to endorse this view.

"He chooses the jobs where his name has been used in vain because they give him a personal interest," he said; "but the personal interest is subsidiary."

It was never quite clear whether the Travelling Circus offended through the careless talk of "Doc" Morane or whether there was an unknown and more vital reason for the events at Arcy-sur-Rhône.

Now, as a rule, systematic breakers of the law are so busy with their own affairs that they do not bother their heads about the operation much less speak slightingly of their own kind. But the Travelling Circus were kings in their sphere, and were superior to the rules which govern lesser crooks. There were three of them: Lijah Hollander, Grab Sitford, and Lee Morane. Li was little and old, a wizened man. Grab was tall and hearty, a bluff, white-haired man, who was, according to his own account, a farmer from Alberta. "Doc" Morane was a tough looker, broad and unprepossessing, ill-mannered. Whether he had ever been anything but a doctor of cards nobody knew or cared.

The Doc was the leader of the gang and had a definite part to play. Little Li Hollander supplied one gentle element, Grab the other; it was the Doc who got rough at the first suggestion of a victim that the game was not straight. Mr. Bliss had expressed the view before that The Ringer controlled the best intelligence department in Europe; apparently he should have included the Western Ocean.

* * * *

The S.S. *Romantic* was sixteen hours from Southampton and the smoke-room was almost empty, for the hour was midnight and wise passengers had gone early to bed, knowing that they would be awakened at dawn by the donkey engines hoisting passengers' baggage into the tender at Cherbourg. A few of the unwise had spent the evening playing poker, and among these was a newspaper man who had been to New York to study the methods of Transatlantic criminals—he was the crime reporter of an important London newspaper. He was a loser of forty pounds before he realised exactly what he was up against, and then he sat out and watched. When the last flushed victim had gone to bed, he had a few words to say to the terrifying Doc and his pained associates.

"Forty pounds, and you can give it back tonight. I don't mind paying for my experience, but I hate paying in money."

"See here"—began the Doc overpoweringly.

"I'm seeing here all right," said the imperturbable scribe: "that's been my occupation all the evening. I saw you palm four decks and it was cleverly done. Now do you mind doing a bit of see-here? There's a Yard man comes on board at daybreak. I'm the crime reporter of the *Megaphone*, and I can give you more trouble than a menagerie of performing fleas. Forty hard-earned pounds—thanks."

The Doc passed the notes across and, dropping for the moment his rôle of bully-in-chief, ordered the drinks.

"You've got a wrong idea about us, but we bear no malice," he said when the drinks came. "The way you were going on I thought you might be that Ringer guy!" he chuckled amiably. "Listen—if The Ringer worked in the State of New York he'd have been framed years ago. He tried to put a bluff on me once, but I called him. That's a fact—am I right, Grab?"

Grab nodded.

"Surely," he said.

The report of this conversation was the only evidence Bliss had that there was any old grudge between The Ringer and the Circus. Very naturally he could not know of the subsequent conversation on the Col de Midi.

"No, I never met him—we had a sort of phone talk. I was staying at the Astoria in London," the Doc went on, his dead-looking face puckered in a smile. "If I'd met him I don't think there would have been any doubt about what'd have happened—eh, Grab?"

The white-haired Grab agreed. He was a living confirmation of all that the Doc asserted, guessed, believed, or theorised.

That was about the whole of the conversation. The Circus left the boat at Cherbourg and travelled south, for this was the season when rich Englishmen leave their native land and go forth in search of the sun. Doc and his friends lingered awhile in Paris, then took separate trains for Nice. Here they stayed in different hotels, packed up a parcel of money which had once been the exclusive property of a bloated Brazilian, missed Monte Carlo—Monte does not countenance competition—and went, by way of Cannes and San Remo, to Milan. Milan drew blank, but there are four easy routes into Switzerland.

"There's a new place up the Rhône Valley full of money," said Doc. "They threw up two new hotels last fall, and they've opened a new bob run that's dangerous to life and limb. The Anglo-Saxon race are sleeping on billiard tables and parking their cash in the pockets."

* * * *

A week later....

"Mr. Pilking" came into the Hotel Ristol, stamping his boots to rid them of the snow, for a blizzard was sweeping down the Rhône Valley and the one street of the little village of Arcy-sur-Rhône was a white chasm through which even the sleighs came with difficulty.

He was a big, florid man, red-faced, white-haired, and he wore a ski-ing suit of blue water-proofed cloth. He had left his skis leaning against the porch of the hotel, but he still carried his long ash sticks.

Mr. Pilking stopped at the desk of the concierge to collect his post, and clumped through the wide lounge to his room. His post was not a heavy one; the guests at the hotel knew him as a business man with large Midland and Northern interests; not even on his holidays could he spare himself, he often said—but his post was very light.

Arcy-sur-Rhône is not a fashionable winter resort. It lies on a shelf of rock, a few thousand feet above the Rhône Valley, and is not sufficiently high to ensure snow, but at an elevation which appeals to people whose hearts are affected by higher altitudes. There is generally a big and select party at the Ristol in January, for Arcy has qualities which not even St. Moritz can rival. The view across the Lake of Geneva is superb, the hotel is so comfortable that its high charges are tolerable, and it can add to its attractions the fact that in all its history it had never consciously harboured an undesirable in the more serious sense of the word. The ski-ing was good, the bob run one of the best in Switzerland; it enjoyed more than its share of snow, and the hotel notice-boards were never disfigured with that hateful notice *Patinage Fermé*.

* * * *

As to whether or not Mr. Sam Welks was altogether desirable, there were several opinions. He was a stoutish man who wore plus-fours all day, never dressed for dinner, talked loudly on all occasions, and was oracular to an offensive degree. Mr Pilking saw him out of the corner of his eye as he passed. He was standing with his back to a pillar, his waving hands glittering in the light of the electroliers—for Mr. Welks wore diamond rings without shame.

"…Gimme London! You can say what you like about scenery and that sort of muck, but where's a better scene than the Embankment on a spring day, eh? You can 'ave your Parises an' Berlins an' Viennas; you can 'ave Venice an' Rome. Take it from me, London's got 'em skinned to death, as the Yankees say. An' New York…! Why, I've made more money in London in a week than some of them so-called millionaires have made in a month o' Sundays! There's more money to be made in dear old London…."

He always talked about money. The dark-haired head waiter, who spoke all languages, used to listen and smile quietly to himself, for he knew London as well as any man. The head waiter was new to Arcy-sur-Rhône; he had only been a week in the place, but he knew every guest in the hotel. He had arrived the same day as Mr. Pilking and his two friends who were waiting for him in his ornate sitting-room.

Doc Morane looked up as Grab came clumping into the room.

"Look at Grab!" he said admiringly. "Gee! I've got to go play that she-ing game—I was a whale at it when I was a kid. Maybe, I'll take Sam out and give him a lesson!"

Old Li Hollander, nodding over an out-of-date visitors' list, woke up and poured himself a glass of ice water.

"We're dining with that Sam Welks man tonight, Grab," he said. "I roped him into a game of bowls after lunch, and he wanted to bet a hundred dollars a game. I could have beaten him fifty, but thought I'd give him a sweetener. That man's clever!"

The Doc was helping himself to whisky.

"I like a clever guy," he said, "but I don't like head waiters who remind me of somebody I've seen before."

Grab looked at his leader sharply.

"All head waiters look that way," he said. "Maybe we've seen him somewhere. These birds travel from hotel to hotel according to the season. Do you remember that guy in Seattle, Doc, the feller you had a fight with when you were running around with Louise Poudalski?"

* * * *

The Doc made a little face. The one person in the world he never wished to be reminded about was Louise Poudalski, and if there was a memory in that episode which grated on him, it was the night in a little Seattle hotel when a German floor waiter had intervened to save Louise from the chastisement which, by the Doc's code—even his drunken code, for he was considerably pickled on that occasion—she deserved. He often used to wonder what had happened to Louise. He had heard about her years ago when he

96

was in New York—she was keeping house for a Chinaman in New Jersey, or was it New Orleans?

"Louise," said Li reminiscently, "was one of the prettiest girls—"

"Shut up about Louise," snarled the Doc. "Are we sweetening this Welks man tonight or are we giving him the axe?"

Grab was for sweetening; but then, in matters of strategy, Grab was always wrong. Li thought that Sam Welks was a "oncer."

"These clever fellows always are. Let 'em win, and they stuff the money into their wallet and tell you they know just when to stop, and that the time to give up playing is when you are on the right side. Soak him tonight and maybe you'll get him tomorrow. The right time to watch a weasel is the first time."

Doc Morane agreed, and Li, dusting the cigar ash from his waistcoat and brushing his thin locks, went down in search of the sacrifice.

Mr. Welks was talking. There seldom was a moment when he was not talking; and Li saw, hovering in the background, the new head waiter, a tall, dark man with a heavy black moustache.

Mr. Welks was in a truculent mood. The manager of the hotel, in the politest possible terms and with infinite tact, had suggested that it would be a graceful compliment to the other guests if he conformed to the ridiculous habit of dressing for dinner.

"Swank!" Mr. Welks was saying to his small and youthful audience—the young people of the hotel got quite a lot of amusement out of studying Mr. Welks at first hand in preparation for giving lifelike imitations of him after supper.

"It's what the Socialists call being class-conscious. It's the only thing I have ever agreed with the Socialists about. I have lived in Leytonstone for twenty-three years man and boy, and I have never dressed for dinner except when I have been going out to swell parties—why should I here, when I am out on an 'oliday? It's preposterous! I pay twenty shillings in the pound wherever I go. I am paying seventy-five francs a day for my soot, and if I can't dress as I like I'll find another hotel. I told this manager—I'm John Blunt. What's the idea of it? Why should I get myself up like a blooming waiter?"

Mr. Hollander thought he saw a faint smile on the face of the head waiter, though apparently he was not listening to the conversation.

"That's my view entirely," said Li. "If I want to dress I dress; if I don't want to dress, I don't dress."

"Exactly," said Mr. Welks, kindling towards his supporter.

* * * *

Li took him by the arm and led him to the bar.

97

"If there's going to be any fuss I'm with you," he said. "And that gentleman, Mr. Pilking, a very nice man indeed, although an American" (Li was born in Cincinnatti) "he holds the same opinion."

They drank together, and Mr. Welks gratefully accepted the invitation, extemporised on the spur of the moment, that he should dine in Mr. Pilking's private room that night.

The Doc and Pilking strolled providentially into the bar to confirm this arrangement, and for an hour the conversation was mainly about Mr. Welks, his building and contractor's business, the money he made during the war, the terrible things that happened to competitors who did not profit by Mr. Welks's example, his distaste of all snobbery and swank, his clever controversies with the Board of Trade, and such other subjects as were, to Mr. Welks, of national interest.

It was after he had drifted off that a curious thing happened which was a little disquieting. The three shared in common a sitting-room, out of which opened on the one side Grab's bedroom and on the other side the Doc's. Li had his bedroom a little farther removed. The Doc went up to his room to make a few necessary preparations for the dinner and the little game which was to follow. He pushed down the lever handle of the sitting-room door, but it did not yield, and at that moment he heard the sound of a chair being overturned. There should have been a light in the sitting-room, but when he stooped to look through the keyhole there was complete darkness.

He went along to the door of his own bedroom and tried that. This, too, was bolted on the inside. The Doc retraced his footsteps to Pilking's room. Here he had better luck. The door was unfastened, and he entered, switching on the light. The door communicating between the bedroom and the sitting-room was wide open. He went in, turned the switch, and walked to the door, which, to his surprise, he found unbolted. He passed through the door leading to his own bedroom, and here he had a similar experience, the door opening readily.

There was no sign of an intruder, no evidence that anything had been disturbed. If the chair had been overturned it had been set on its feet again. He opened the door of the long cupboard, which might conceal an intruder, but, save for his clothes suspended on hangers, it was empty.

Returning through the sitting-room, he went out into the corridor. As he did so he saw a man come, apparently from the stairs, stand for a moment as if in doubt, and then, catching sight of the Doc, turn swiftly and disappear—not, however, before Doc Morane had recognised the dark-haired head waiter.

* * * *

Very thoughtfully he returned to his apartment and made another search. Nothing, so far as he could see, had been disturbed. He locked the doors and opened a suitcase which stood on a small pedestal. There must have been over a hundred packs of cards in that case, each fastened with a rubber band and each representing half an hour's intensive arrangement. These had no appearance of having been disturbed. He relocked the grip and went slowly back to his companions, and at the earliest opportunity told them what had happened.

"Somebody was in the room," he said, "and I pretty well know who that somebody was."

Elijah was obviously worried.

"Maybe that waiter is an hotel 'tec," he said. "Up at St. Moritz the Federal people sent a couple of 'tecs into one of the hotels and pinched the Mosser crowd."

Mr. Sam Welks did not go to his host's room that night unprepared for the little game that was to follow. It was Li who had suggested it. "Mr. Pilking was not particularly keen," he said. He didn't like playing for money; one wasn't sure if the people who lost could really afford to lose.

The talkative Sam had bridled at the suggestion—this was over cocktails before dinner.

"Speakin' for meself," he said, "I don't worry about people losin'. If they can't afford to lose they shouldn't play. That foreign-lookin' waiter feller had the nerve to tell me not to play cards with strangers. I told him to mind his own business. I never heard such cheek in my life! If anybody can catch me, good luck to 'em. But they couldn't. I've met some of the cleverest crooks in London, an' they've all had a cut at me."

He chuckled at the thought.

"Bless your life! When a man's knocked about in the world as I have it takes a clever feller to best him. See what I mean? It's an instinct with me, knowin' the wrong 'uns. I remember once when I was stayin' at Margate...."

They let him talk, but each of the three was thinking furiously. It was Doc Morane who put their thoughts into words.

"That waiter was frisking the apartment," he said, "and that means no good to anybody. We'll skin this rabbit and get away tomorrow if he looks like squealing—"

"He'll not squeal," said the saintly Li, who was the psychologist of the party. "He wouldn't admit he'd been had. The most he'll do is to ask for a No. 2 seance, but I'm all for getting while the road's good. This is going to be one large killing!"

* * * *

99

The dinner in the little salon was a great success. Grab, who was something of a gourmet, had ordered it with every care.

Under the mellowing influence of '15 Steinberger Cabinet, Mr. Welks grew expansive. He wore his noisiest plus-fours, and, as a further gesture of defiance against the conventions, a soft-collared shirt of purple silk.

"You've got to take me as I am," he said, "as other people have done before. I don't put on side and I don't expect other people to. My 'ome in Leytonstone is Liberty 'All—I don't ask people who their fathers was—were. I could have been a knight if I'd wanted to be, but that kind of thing doesn't appeal to me. Titles—bah!"

The time came when the dinner table was wheeled out into the corridor and a green-covered table was brought into the centre of the room. Again Mr. Pilking made his conventional protest.

"I don't like playing for money. Although I know you two gentleman, I don't know Mr. Welks, and I've always made a rule never to play with strangers."

He said this probably a hundred times a year, and it never failed to provoke the marked victim.

"Look here, mister," said Welks hotly, "if my money's not good enough for you, you needn't play! If it comes to that, I don't know you. Money talks—hear mine!"

He thrust his hands into his pockets and took out a thick roll of Swiss bills, and from a pocket cunningly placed on the inside of his plus-fours, a thicker wad of Bank of England notes.

"The Swiss are milles—which means a thousand—an' these good old English notes are for a hundred. Now let's see yours!"

With a perfect assumption of hesitancy, Mr. Pilking produced a goodly pile and his companions followed suit.

For the first quarter of an hour the luck went in the direction of Mr. Welks—which was the usual method of the Travelling Circus.

Unseen by any, Doc Morane "palmed" a new pack. The substitution was made all the easier by the fact that Welks was separating the larger from the smaller notes which represented his inconsiderable winnings.

"Cut," said the Doc, offering the pack.

"Run 'em." replied Mr. Welks professionally.

* * * *

Something went wrong with the hand. Welks should have held four queens and the Doc four kings. These latter appeared in Doc Morane's hand all right, and the betting began.

Li threw in his hand when the bidding reached six hundred pounds. Grab retired at eight hundred. The Doc brought the bidding to a thousand.

100

"And two hundred," said Mr. Welks recklessly.

Doc Morane made a rapid calculation. This man was good for a few thousands if he was gentled.

"I'll see you," he said, and nearly collapsed when the triumphant Mr. Welks laid down four aces.

Li took the pack from the table, and with a lightning movement dropped it to his lap as he slipped a new pack into its place. Li was the cleverest of all broad-men at this trick.

"Run 'em," said the Doc as the pack was offered to him.

This time there could be no mistake. The four knaves came to him, and he knew by Li's nod and Grab's yawn that they each held one ace, king and queen. Mr. Welks drew two cards—which was exactly the number he should have drawn. The Doc knew that he now held two kings and three tens.

They bid up to eight hundred, which was more than any sane man would bet on a "full house."

"I'll see you," growled Doc Morane.

Mr. Welks laid down a small straight flush.

"You'll have to take a cheque," said the Doc when he recovered.

"I'll take the cash you've got and a cheque for the rest," said Welks. He was a picture of fatuous joy. "I'm a business man, old boy, but I know something about poker, eh?"

That ended the party; they were too clever not to accept his invitation to the bar for a celebration. The three went upstairs together and Doc Morane locked the salon door.

"Somebody was in here before dinner, planting new decks of cards," he said. "Did you lamp the head waiter? I'll fix that bird!"

"What are we going to do?" asked Li fretfully. "Do we get or stay?"

"We're not leaving till we get that money and more," said Grab savagely. "What do you say, Doc?"

Doc Morane nodded.

"Me an' Welks are like brothers," he said significantly. "We're going she-ing on the Midi slopes tomorrow morning, and I'll hook him for tonight. You fellows stay home and fix those cards."

* * * *

A little railway carried a small and cold party to the ski-ing fields early the next morning. Because the upper stretches of the line were snowed under the party descended on the Col de Midi, which is a razor-backed ridge which mounts steeply up to the precipice face of the Midi Massif.

Mr. Welks was no mean exponent of the art, and led his companion up the snowy slopes. And all the time he sang loudly and untunefully the vul-

101

gar song of the moment.

The head waiter had not been in the train. Once or twice the Doc looked round to make sure. He saw a Swiss guide signalling frantically, but nobody seemed coming their way, and when Mr. Welks pulled up after an hour's laborious climb they were alone.

"You're not a good skier, my friend," he said pleasantly.

The Doc wiped his perspiring forehead and growled something.

"A little farther," said Mr. Welks, and went on.

The Doc noticed that he went tenderly along the crest of a snowy cornice, but did not understand why until he had passed and, looking back, saw that they had passed a snowy bridge over a deep chasm.

"Dangerous, eh?" Mr. Welks smiled gleefully. "You can take off your skis."

"Why?" asked the Doc, frowning.

"Because I ask you."

The Doc took off his skis: he invariably did what he was told to when the teller covered him with a Browning pistol.

Mr. Welks lifted the skis and threw them into the chasm.

"On the other side of this ridge is Italy," he said pleasantly. "That is where I am going. What will happen to you I don't know. It is impossible to walk back. Perhaps the head waiter—who is the best detective in Switzerland—will rescue you. He was going to arrest you, anyway. By the way, it was I who planted the cards last night."

"Who are you?" The Doc's white face was whiter yet.

Mr. Welks smiled.

"My wife had a little friend in Seattle—one Louise Poudalski. Remember her?"

Before Doc Morane could reply, The Ringer was flying down the Italian slope, his skis raising snow like steam....

102

Chapter 11

The Escape Of Mr. Bliss

There was an incident on the Oxford and Henley Road which may be recorded as a matter of interest, since it marked the introduction of Superintendent Bliss to Silas Maginnis.

Mr. Bliss, who was (despite certain poetical tendencies) a great realist, always believed that the name "Silas" was the imagining of story-writers. All his life he had never met a human being who bore such a name; never once had he written "Silas" on any charge sheet.

Naturally, he knew that Silas Maginnis had arrived in the neighbourhood. The ruined chapel of Chapel-Stanstead, a veritable Norman relic which, to the discredit of the county, had been allowed to fall into decay, was now made whole, thanks to the generosity of an American philanthropist—and to a variety of other causes.

It had stood in a swampy marsh, but when the Wollingford Brick Company had begun operations on an adjoining property, and the Wollingford District Council had made certain improvements to the banking of a little river which ran through the shallow valley of Wollingford, the land became automatically drained, and there stood high and dry the four walls of the chapel, a couple of arches intact and eight little pillars.

Said the vicar of Wollingford: "You should see the chapel, Mr. Bliss: it is rather beautiful, and I don't suppose that it cost more than a thousand to restore. Mr. Mountford—he's the American who paid for the restoration—has fixed up a caretaker who is almost as interesting as the chapel! My curate is holding a service there next Sunday. Go along and see the chapel—and Silas!"

But Superintendent Bliss was not a churchman. He went to Wollingford at weekends solely for the purpose of recreation.

He liked to spend his weekends out of town. He had a cottage between Oxford and Newbury and some forty-five acres of indifferent land which he inherited from an aunt. In addition, he had the shooting rights over a couple of hundred acres. This latter cost him no more than a gun licence, for the owner of the shoot was a wealthy and grateful man to whom Bliss had once rendered a very important service.

On Saturday mornings the detective could be seen, with a gun under his arm and a lurcher at his heels, loafing along likely hedges, a pipe between his bearded lips and an ancient and battered hat on the back of his head. Here he touched a new life and found new interests which helped to dispel the cobwebs with which his drab work at Scotland Yard encumbered his brain.

Sometimes he met the vicar of Wollingford, an elderly man but a deadly shot, and occasionally he foregathered with Mr. Selby-Grout, a middle-aged man who had recently acquired Wollingford Hall and the lordship of the manor. He was a taciturn man of fifty, grey-haired and heavy-moustached, whose principal occupation in life was shooting.

Sometimes, as they sat in the pale spring sunlight discussing lunch, Bliss would talk of his work, and if the question of Mr. X. arose it was because a foreign bank in which Mr. Selby-Grout had an interest had been victimised.

The lord of the manor was rather scornful on the subject of restored chapels.

"It's a pity these damned Americans haven't something better to do with their money," he growled. "I haven't seen the church, but the other day I saw the half-witted verger, or sexton, or whatever he is…. He has Church Cottage—the Yankee bought that, too. Silas something. Have a look at him. He's madder than the Yankee who put him there."

A week after this Mr. Bliss met Silas Maginnis.

* * * *

Mr. Mander strolled into his chief's office on the following Friday afternoon, and he took with him an elaborately drawn map of England and a brand new theory about The Ringer.

The day being what it was, Mr. Bliss had no desire to read maps or examine theories; his little car was waiting in the courtyard, and, in addition to a suitcase in which he had packed the newest book that a subscription library could supply, the car carried a market basket in which was packed a weekend's supply of provisions.

Being independent of trains and timetables, he settled down with resignation to listen.

"Fire ahead, but keep it short," he said.

Inspector Mander spread the map.

"For three months nothing has been heard or seen of The Ringer," he said impressively. "My view is that he is still in England—"

"Your view is probably supported by the fact that I had a letter from him yesterday. I seem to remember that I told you," said Bliss wearily. "I presume that all these crosses in black ink on the map are intended to show the scenes of his activities, and the crosses in red ink where he is most likely to appear next."

"They are all near a railway station—" began Mr. Mander, anxious to avert the demolition of his "theory."

"Everything is near a railway station in England," said his superior coldly.

He glanced at the map, and was irritably amused to note that a certain village in Oxfordshire bore an extra large red cross.

"Why Wollingford?" he asked.

Here Mr. Mander could elaborate his theory.

"You have had three letters from him recently," he said, with the deliberation of one who is revealing a great discovery. "One was posted in the Paddington district, one was posted at Reading, one was posted at Cheltenham. I have been studying these postmarks very carefully, and I have compared them with a time-table. They all coincide with the theory that this man is operating from somewhere near Oxford."

Bliss glanced at the figures on the sheet of paper which his subordinate placed before him. It was true that he had received three letters written by the portable typewriter which was part of The Ringer's baggage.

One had warned him about the impending departure of a gentleman who had swindled a very large number of shareholders, and who was packing his bag to catch the Air Mail when Bliss descended on him; another was a sympathetic inquiry after the health of the superintendent, who had been knocked over in Whitehall by a motor-lorry without any serious damage; and the third bore reference to some statement attributed to Bliss in connection with one of The Ringer's most daring exploits—"a statement which I am sure that a man with your peculiar sense of fairness could not have made," said the writer politely.

And, since all the documents in the case of The Ringer went automatically to Inspector Mander, he had seen these three letters, and, less from their contents than their superscription, had evolved his great idea.

Bliss pushed the note back and shook his head.

"Your time-table tells me nothing except that you are most industrious when you are pursuing dud clues," he said crushingly. But it took a lot to crush Mr. Mander.

* * * *

At the moment Scotland Yard was less interested in The Ringer than in a gang which was engaged in the forging and uttering of letters of credit on an extensive scale.

The master criminal is supposed to be a figment of the novelist's imagination—and usually he is; but somewhere in England was a brilliant criminal who, with the aid of a small printing press, was literally coining money.

Complaints had flowed into Scotland Yard for eighteen months: they came from places as far apart as Constantinople and Stockholm. Twice, the agents of Mr. X. had been caught, but the police were unable to trace the head of the business, except that all the evidence pointed to the fact that he operated from England and worked through a super-agent in Paris.

Bliss was thinking of Mr. X. as his little car sped down the Great West Road. There had come to him that week the faintest hint of a whisper that one Elizabeth Hineshaft might lead him to the forger; but Elizabeth, when she was interviewed at Holloway Prison, had shown no enthusiastic desire to offer information. She was rather a pretty woman, and he knew no more of her friendships than that she had many.

She ran with Bossy Clewsher, a great organiser of spieling clubs, who had made more than a fortune out of high-class gambling hells in Mayfair and Regent's Park, and would have made another when he opened a similar club in the very heart of the West End if it had not been for the activities of Bliss.

He arrested Bossy one unpleasant night and took Elizabeth in the same net. Unfortunately for this lady, she was in possession of a small portfolio —it was between overlay and mattress.

It is rather difficult to explain what that portfolio contained, or how she came to possess it. One does not wish to cast reflections upon the character of under-secretaries of State, especially middle-aged under-secretaries who ought to have known better. She was a very attractive girl, and even budding statesmen do incomprehensibly stupid things.

There would have been no harm in it if the papers in the portfolio were plans of a new submarine or a scheme for attacking the Russian fleet, or such things as are usually stolen in stories.

The documents actually contained in that flat leather wallet were letters written by the leaders of two parties dealing with a possible fusion of party interests. Mr. Z. was the intermediary and had been promised Cabinet rank if he pulled off the deal, so that when he discovered his loss he was not unnaturally agitated. His advertisement:

LOST: Probably in a taxicab between Birdcage Walk and Maida Vale, a red leather portfolio containing papers of no value to anybody but the owner, etc.

appeared in every newspaper

* * * *

Mr. Bliss found the portfolio and unwittingly became involved in the highest kind of politics.

Lawbreakers are not severely punished for stealing Cabinet secrets, and it is quite possible that Elizabeth might never have had that particular piece of stealing brought up against her. Only, with the portfolio was found a flat case containing a large number of small phials containing a narcotic favoured by drug addicts, and, with this evidence that she had a fairly large clientele.

She was an old offender, though young in years. There were seven distinct counts to her indictment, and when these were supported by a record of five convictions her sentence was inevitable. She was sent down for the term of five years, and when somebody in the public gallery heard the Judge deliver judgment he burst into tears.

"Find the weeper," said Bliss after this had been reported to him; but the quest was unsuccessful.

The whisperers of the underworld hinted in their vague way that Elizabeth was well beloved. She certainty lived in the style of one who had unlimited sources of income; her jewels were worth thousands, and her flat was furnished regardless of cost.

If you ask why, in these circumstances, she bothered her head to peddle dope, there is this reply: that criminals are all a little mad. Did not the notorious Al Finney, with twenty thousand in the bank, go down to the shades for a cheap swindle that could not have netted him more than fifty pounds?

* * * *

Bliss was musing on these queer inconsistencies when his car drew up at a small garage on the outskirts of Colnbrook. He invariably stopped here for a weekend supply of petrol. The garage keeper knew him and came out with a letter in his hand.

"It was left here an hour ago," he said.

"For me?" demanded Bliss in surprise, and then, when he saw the typewritten envelope: "Who left this?"

The man did not know. He had found the note stuck to the door with a glass-headed pin, such as photographers use to hang up films.

He tore open the letter. It consisted of six typewritten lines:

Take the Reading road. It is a long way round, but safer. I don't exactly know what they are preparing for you, but it is something unpleasant. And I don't want you to die.

The Ringer! There was no doubt about that typewriting. Bliss smiled grimly. So Mander had been more or less right. The Ringer's headquarters were somewhere in this neighbourhood.

When his petrol tank was filled and three extra tins loaded into the back he resumed his journey. West of Maidenhead he had two alternative routes:

he could pass through Henley; he could follow the main road to Reading, as The Ringer advised. He chose Henley and whatever danger lay beyond.

It was quite dark now, and, clear of Henley town, he switched on his headlights, stopped the car, and, taking an automatic from his handbag, laid it on the seat beside him.

Wollingford lies off the main road. He came to the place where he had to turn and slowed down. Invariably he came this way. The road was narrow and for a mile was between high hedges. Presently his headlamps revealed the little Norman chapel, and in its shadow the tiny cottage where the "crazy" caretaker lived. He passed this, followed the sharp turn of the lane, and then suddenly his foot went down on the brake.

Standing in the middle of the road, and in the glare of the headlamps, was a figure with outstretched arms. Bliss stared at the twisted face, the wide eyes, the foolishly-smiling mouth, and his hand dropped to his gun. For a second he experienced a little thrill of apprehension, but the man was unarmed.

"What do you want?" he demanded, and stepped down from the car.

The stupid face contorted into a leering smile.

"He told me to stop you, master…the big man on the bicycle. He took me from my cottage and said, 'Stand there and stop him.'"

His voice was uncannily shrill, and when he chuckled Bliss felt a cold shiver run down his spine.

"He came on a bicycle…it made noises like a devil…bing-bang! And he said, 'Stay there—I cannot cut the wire!'"

"The wire?"

The strange figure turned, and, pointing into the darkness, chuckled again.

Bliss found an electric torch and walked down the road. He had not far to go. A stout wire had been fastened across the road a few feet from the ground. It was just high enough to miss the little windscreen and catch the driver.

When he walked back to the car the mad-looking caretaker had vanished. Getting into the car, he backed it until he came to the caretaker's cottage, and, getting down, he knocked at the door. There was no answer. Bliss was puzzled and more than a little perturbed.

He drove on to where the wire was stretched, stopped long enough to cut it and throw the loose end over the hedge, and reached his own cottage a very thoughtful man.

He locked all the doors carefully before he retired and slept till late the following morning. Almost the first person he saw after breakfast was Mr. Selby-Grout. He was leaning over the cottage gate, a big pipe between his strong teeth, his gun resting against the gate.

"Hullo!" he boomed. "What about Henfield Wood?"

It was only then that Bliss remembered that he had accepted an invitation to shoot over the big man's land.

On the way across the fields he related what had happened the previous night, and Mr. Selby-Grout listened with a frown.

"I should think the crazy brute put the wire there himself," he said. "I saw him this morning snooping round my house—in fact, he was in my library when I came down. How on earth he got there I don't know. He said he'd made a mistake and came through the wrong door. He often comes up to the house to beg food from the servants. By gad, there he is!"

Bliss turned his head and looked. They were nearing the plantation which was known as Henfield Wood, and he caught a glimpse of a figure disappearing behind a belt of bush.

"There he goes!"

A man was running across the open towards a cut road which formed a boundary to the property. Bliss saw him leap a low hedge and disappear, apparently into the earth.

"I'd like to take a shot at the devil!" growled the owner of the land.

It was some time before he recovered his equanimity. They walked a little way into the wood, and then both men loaded.

"I'll bet he's frightened away every feather of game," said Mr. Selby-Grout; and then, most unexpectedly: "Did you ever hear of a woman called Elizabeth Hineshaft?"

"Yes—I see you've been reading the newspapers," smiled Bliss. "I got her a term of penal servitude this week."

"Oh, you did, did you?"

Click!

It was the sound of a gun-hammer falling, but Bliss did not look round.

Click!

"What's wrong?"

Selby-Grout was staring at the gun in his hand. His face was white and streaming with perspiration; the hand that held the gun was shaking.

"I don't know...that fellow rattled me," he said hoarsely.

He was trembling from head to foot.

"For God's sake, what is wrong with you?"

The man shook his head.

"Let's go back."

They walked for a long time in complete silence.

"I'd give a lot of money to know if he is working with The Ringer," said Bliss, speaking his thoughts aloud.

The gun dropped from the nerveless hand of his companion. For a second he swayed as though he were about to fall, and Bliss gripped him by the arm.

"The Ringer!" His breath came in gasps. "...my library—he was there—chequebook on table—!"

At eleven-thirty that morning a handsome-looking limousine drew up before the Leadenhall Street branch of the Western Counties Bank, and a man in the livery of a chauffeur interviewed the manager. He had a letter bearing the note-heading of Wollingford Hall.

The letter was written in Mr. Selby-Grout's characteristic handwriting. He needed thirty-three thousand pounds in cash. It was not unusual that Mr. Selby-Grout should make large withdrawals. The cheque which accompanied the letter was duly honoured.

The manager of the Western Counties afterwards remarked to his assistant that Mr. Selby-Grout's account was hardly worth keeping. No sooner did big sums come in than they were withdrawn. Subsequently he repeated this to Superintendent Bliss, and showed him some significant figures, but this was after Bliss returned to Scotland Yard and found a long typewritten letter awaiting him.

My dear Bliss,—

You are under a great obligation to me—twice have I saved your life! Honestly, I did think that your Mr. X. was waiting to shoot you on the Henley road. You see, I know all about his romantic love affair with Elizabeth.

I only discovered the wire too late to remove it. I guessed that he was staging a shooting accident; for a week he has been rehearsing that accidental shooting—holding his gun first one way and then another.

Eventually I think he decided to shoot you while the gun was under his arm. He became quite an adept at this method, and you will find certain trees in the wood simply peppered with shot.

So sure was I that I took a haversack full of dud cartridges with me this (Saturday) morning to his library—he keeps his guns and cartridges in that noble apartment—and made an exchange. Otherwise you would be dead.

I also borrowed a blank cheque—the notepaper I have had for a week.

Yes, I was the American who restored the chapel—by letter. I appointed myself caretaker. I had to live in the neighbourhood without exciting suspicion. I have been after Mr. X.—whose real name is Whotby—for the greater part of a year. You will find his printing press in his dressing-room.

Why do I betray my fellow criminal? Does dog eat dog, you ask? Alas! he does! It is for your dear sake that I give him away—your life

110

is too precious to risk, Think well of me, your benefactor.

P.S.—I should not have saved Mander.

Mr. Bliss was not as flattered by these gracious references to his life as he might have been. On the other hand, he agreed about Mander.

Chapter 12

The Man With the Beard

The trouble with Mr. Bliss, from the point of view of the Yard, was that he tried to do too much himself. He had, moreover, a furtive and secret method of working, consulted nobody, and seldom informed even his immediate superior that he was taking on some especial task until the moment was ripe for an arrest.

An example of his methods was the case of the brothers Steinford. London had become flooded with forged ten-shilling notes—ten-shilling notes being much easier to pass than the pound variety. He took the case himself, and immediately it vanished as a subject of discussion; when the conferences were called and the forged bills came up for examination, Bliss would content himself with saying: "Oh, yes, I'm seeing to that." No further comment was made.

He took a journey or two into the Midlands, went down into Wales to interview a man serving a sentence, and, with his assistance, found a gentleman named Poggy, who kept a baked potato-can and lived in East Greenwich.

But the solution of the mystery was never revealed. Nobody was arrested, and when the forgery was mentioned in Mr. Mander's private office he would look at his sycophantic sergeant, and they would raise their eyebrows together and smile. All of which indicated a deep disparagement of Mr. Bliss and his methods.

In the Rowley murder case it was the same. Bliss didn't bother to look for the tall, dark man who had been seen in the neighbourhood of Mr. Rowley's house, but scoured London to find an old carpet slipper, the fellow of that which had been left behind in the kitchen of Mr. Rowley's house on the night of the murder.

In this case, of course, he was successful; but, as Mr. Mander so often said, it is the exception which proves the rule.

* * * *

There appeared in the pages of a popular weekly periodical an article entitled: "Can The Ringer Be Caught?" Its author was described as "the greatest living authority upon this super-criminal." His name was modestly withheld. It described certain exploits of Henry Arthur Milton, and dealt with the failure of those who were responsible for his capture. One passage ran:

There is no doubt that those engaged in the search are either stale or inefficient. Contemporaneously with his activities, a strange inertia seems to have settled on the officers in charge of the various cases.

Now, every man has his favourite word, and, the less literate he is, the more frequently it is employed. Mr. Bliss, who had read many reports written by the officer, knew that "contemporaneously" was a great pet with Inspector Mander. If he had a second fancy it was for "inertia," and these words occurred many times in the article.

He rang the bell, and the messenger came. "Ask Mr. Mander to see me, please," he said.

Inspector Mander arrived cheerfully, but at the sight of the periodical spread out on the superintendent's desk he changed colour.

"Have you read this article, Mander?"

Mr. Mander cleared his throat.

"No," he said boldly.

"An interesting one—you should take it home and study it," said the icy voice of Superintendent Bliss. "It is full of queer English, and is obviously written by a man who, in addition to being a fool and disloyal to his superiors, is also extremely illiterate."

Bliss did not look up, yet a furtive glance told him that Mr. Mander's face had gone a deep red.

"He says, amongst other things," Bliss went on, "that—well, I'll read it:

The Ringer is not so clever as people think he is. By a series of lucky chances, he has escaped detection; but, sooner or later, the one man at Scotland Yard whose name perhaps is less known to the public than the officer who is associated with The Ringer and his nefarious acts will bring him to justice.

"I gather from this rather involved sentence that there is a super-intelligence at Scotland Yard. Do you happen to know whose it is?"

"No," said Mander loudly.

Bliss folded the paper, picked it up, as though it were some noxious and evil-smelling thing, with the tips of his finger and thumb, and dropped it carefully into the wastepaper basket.

"It isn't the paper," he explained, "it's the article that makes me sick. I can only say that whoever wrote that article is a very bold man. It is a challenge to The Ringer, and I have never known him to ignore a challenge. I shall be interested to see if the writer is still alive at the end of next week because it contains some very rude references both to The Ringer's courage and his genius."

There was a silence, which, with an effort, Mr. Mander broke.

"Who do you think wrote it?" he asked, a little huskily.

Bliss shook his head.

"Obviously an hysterical woman," he said icily, fished the periodical from the wastepaper basket, and handed it to his subordinate. "Read it—it will give you a laugh."

* * * *

There were, apparently, people who agreed with the writer of the article. Mr. Mander lived in Maida Vale, and it was his practice to travel home by Tube. Police-Constable Olivan, who stepped into the Tube compartment with him one night, was among the number. He grinned, touched his helmet, and, with an apology, sat down by the side of the inspector.

Mr. Mander was not averse from being saluted by policemen: he was one of those men who believe that detective-inspectors should carry a gold badge or something equally distinguishing, so that common individuals should not rub elbows with him without realising the honour his presence gave them.

"Do you mind if I smoke, sir?"

Police-Constable Olivan was obviously going off duty; he carried a rolled waterproof cape between his knees, and he took the liberty, after consulting the inspector, to light a clay pipe.

"Oh, yes, sir, I recognised you; I've seen you in several big cases," he said, a smile on his rubicund face. "It's a funny thing—I was only talking to our sergeant this morning about you, sir, if I might be so bold."

Mr. Mander inclined his head graciously to indicate that Police-Constable Olivan could be as bold as he liked, so long as the talk was complimentary.

"I read a bit in the paper—I forget the name of it—about this Ringer, and I said to my sergeant: 'I'll bet the gentleman that feller means is Mr. Mander.'"

"I haven't read the article, constable," said Mr. Mander.

"You ought to, sir," said the other earnestly. "It's the talk of our division. Do you know what I think, sir, if I might say so without being disrespectful to my superiors? I think a flat-footed policeman could catch that Ringer better than some of the people that's taken an 'and in it."

"I wouldn't say that," demurred Mr. Mander.

The constable nodded.

"Naturally you wouldn't, sir; I understand the police service very well. I've been twenty-three years a constable. They offered to make me a sergeant when I'd done seven years' street-duty, but I wouldn't look at it.

"I haven't got the education," he added, "and I can't be bothered to go to school with a parcel of young policemen."

"So you think that you could catch The Ringer, eh?"

Mander looked at the police officer with an amused smile.

"Good Lord, no, sir!" the man hastened to excuse himself. "All I say is that if I was assistant to a gentleman like you—somebody that gave me confidence—we'd run him to earth in a week—if you'll excuse my saying 'we'."

He took out his pipe, looked round the compartment as though to be sure that there was nobody near enough to hear him, and bending towards Mr. Mander, said in a low, confidential voice: "I don't mind telling you, sir, there's a man keeping a money-lender's business near where I live who might be The Ringer. He's only been in the place about two months; he's seldom at home, and when he does come home it's always at night."

"What does he look like?" asked Mander, interested.

"He's got a little beard, rather like Mr. Bliss, sir. I don't even know whether he's a money-lender. I know he's got the premises that old Isaacstein used to have: but there it is!"

Constable Olivan grew confidential about himself. He had been married seventeen years, and nobody had a better wife, unless, he added hastily, Mr. Mander was married. Mr. Mander denied that happy state.

It was easy to see that Police-Constable Olivan was tremendously interested in the high politics of the police force. Mander glowed under the enthusiastic admiration of his subordinate.

"If I'd had any sense," said the policeman, "I'd have gone into the C.I.D. years ago. It's too late now. It fairly makes me writhe when I see fellows getting away with it as they are every day. Look at those ten-shilling forgers: nothing's been done about it! In our division they say that there's going to be a lot of changes at Scotland Yard, and, with all due respect, sir, I think it's about time."

Mr. Mander thought so too.

"Where is this house where the mysterious Ringer lives?" he asked flippantly.

The constable drew a little plan on the palm of his hand.

"I'll ride on with you and take a look at the place," said Mr. Mander, and Olivan nearly dissolved with gratification.

"If any of my mates saw me with you, sir," he said humorously as they left the station, "it'd be a rare feather in my cap! But only two of our division live round here. It's hard to find a house…."

As they trudged through the dark streets he enlarged upon every policeman's grievance, which is mainly confined to the question of pay and allowances.

They came at last to a narrow crescent, where houses stood shoulder to shoulder. They must have been built in the 'sixties, and they bore the unmistakable stamp of the 'sixty architects' atrocious minds. Flights of stone stairs led up to the front doors; there was a little narrow basement, protected by railings; and above the level reached by the stone stairs was another floor.

"That's my house." The police-constable pointed. "When I say it's my house, I mean I've got three rooms there." He thought a moment and added a kitchenette; he was evidently not a fast thinker. "If you'll come along, sir, I'll show you the other place."

Half-way along the crescent the houses were divided by a narrow lane, about wide enough to take the wheels of a cart.

"That's the house." He pointed to the corner premises. "And this is what always strikes me."

He led the way down the passage. On the right was a wall the height of a tall man's chin, and over this Mander commanded an uninterrupted view of a back garden. At the end of the garden was a solid-looking building which, Olivan explained, comprised the premises of a firm of electrical instrument makers, the entrance being in the street running parallel to the crescent.

Except for one window set upon an upper floor, the back of the premises which showed on to the garden of the mysterious stranger was black.

"See that window?" said Olivan impressively. "I'll tell you something about that, sir. I came home rather late one night, suffering from insomnia or indigestion, as the case may be, and I had a walk round and a smoke. I come along this very passage, and what do you think I saw? A ladder up to that window! That's funny, I thought. I didn't know that this fellow had moved into the house then. I continued my stroll, and when I come back the ladder wasn't there!"

He said this dramatically. Mr. Mander scratched his chin.

"Electrical instrument makers, eh?" he said thoughtfully. "I'd like to have a little private investigation here, constable. What time are you off duty tomorrow night?"

"Seven o'clock, sir. It's about eight by the time I get home."

"Could you meet me at the end of this street at half-past eight?" suggested Mander. "I don't want you to be in uniform—you understand?"

"Quite, sir," said the constable gravely. "You want the whole thing to be private."

"And I don't want you to mention the fact to any of your friends, your sergeant, or your inspector. In fact, this is a private matter between ourselves. If I pull off anything, you may be sure you won't be the loser."

"Very good, sir."

Constable Olivan saluted. He insisted upon walking with Mander back to the end of the street.

"There's a lot of bad characters around here, sir, and, although I know you're quite capable of looking after yourself, I shouldn't like anything unpleasant to happen in our neighbourhood." Which was very thoughtful of him.

* * * *

When Mander got to the office next morning he found Bliss had already arrived and had twice sent for him. With a little sinking of heart, his mind instantly flew to his ill-timed literary effort; but Superintendent Bliss had evidently forgotten all about that unhappy lapse.

"The Ringer is in London," he said. "I had a phone message from a callbox this morning, and, although I was able to locate the box in the Kingsland Road, I haven't been able to track the gentleman. I want to warn you."

Mr. Mander was startled.

"Warn me, sir? Why?"

"Because I have an idea that you are immediately concerned," said Bliss grimly. "If you feel you'd like to go after this gentleman, you're at perfect liberty to do so. I have a couple of cases which will occupy all my time and probably take me out of town a good deal."

Mr. Mander smiled.

"I don't know that there's much to go on," he said. "A telephone message from the north of London doesn't give us a great deal of assistance."

Bliss looked up at the ceiling.

"I seem to remember reading an article in which the writer said that the big mistake they were making at Scotland Yard was in waiting for definite clues. I also seem to remember that there was some talk of anticipating The Ringer's movements and working out a theory as to what he would do next."

Mander coughed.

"Yes, I read the article," he said awkwardly. "Nonsense, I call it."

"Damned nonsense, I should call it," said Bliss; and for a moment his subordinate hated him, for he loved that little article, the composition of which had occupied so much of his time.

He considered the matter all the morning. The telephone message had come from North London, and that fitted with Constable Olivan's theory. He might be wildly guessing; at the same time, luck runs in curious grooves, and who knew if that stolid man might not be the instrument for bringing Mander's name prominently before the world as the single-handed captor of The Ringer?

It was an old trick of The Ringer's, too, to call up Scotland Yard.

* * * *

When Mander met his new assistant that night he had half formulated a working theory.

Constable Olivan in mufti was less imposing than Constable Olivan in uniform. He wore a purplish suit, a silver watch guard decorated with athletic medals, and on his feet a pair of white gymnasium shoes.

"He's in the 'ouse, sir." Olivan was in a state of excitement. "He come up in a taxicab and let himself in with a key. I'll tell you something, sir: I've been making a few inquiries in the neighbourhood, and that house is practically unfurnished.

"He's got one little bedroom where he sleeps, and all the other rooms are empty. They took old Isaacstein's money-lending sign away yesterday, so he's not in that business. Isaacstein was the fellow who was pinched for receiving about two months ago."

They made their way to the passage and took up a position near the wall. After an hour their vigilance was rewarded. There came the click of a door opening, and presently Mr. Mander espied a dark figure stealing through the garden towards the building at the end. He waited some time, then heard a thud, like the sound of a door closing.

Ten minutes passed, and then Mander, with the assistance of the constable, climbed over the wall and went stealthily in the direction of the building.

There was nobody in sight. The man, whoever he was, had vanished, and after a little search Mander discovered where he had gone. Near the wall of the instrument maker's little factory was a wooden trapdoor, and when Mander tried this he found it was unbolted. He peered down into the darkness, but could see and could certainly hear nothing. Replacing the trap, he returned to his companion.

"He may be just an ordinary burglar," he said. "I want to make sure before reporting."

He gave Olivan his private address and telephone number, and the constable volunteered to keep watch until two o'clock in the morning, after which, "nature being what it is," as he reluctantly confessed, he could not maintain the surveillance.

It was a little after eleven when Mr. Mander reached his home, and he had hardly entered the hall of the respectable boarding-house where he had his residence when the telephone bell rang.

"For you, Mr. Mander," said the landlady, bustling out from the sitting-room which she called an office.

Mander went in. It was Olivan's excited voice.

"Excuse me, sir. He come out of the house and I trailed him. He went to one of the public telephones in the street and I heard him call Victoria 7000

—isn't that Scotland Yard?"

"Yes, yes," said Mander impatiently. "Did you hear what he said?"

"No, sir. He shut the door after he gave the number."

Mander thought quickly.

"Ring me up in ten minutes' time. I'm going to get on to the Yard."

In a few minutes he was connected with his own office, and after a little delay found somebody who could give him information.

"Yes, there's been a message through from The Ringer tonight. I don't know how genuine it was. I wrote it out and, as a matter of fact, I was just going to call you up to give it to you. I'll get it now."

"What was it about?" asked Mander impatiently. "Anyway, it doesn't matter, so long as you're sure it was from The Ringer. Do you know where the call came from?"

The officer in charge had taken the precaution of locating the message. It must have been the very box from which the spying Olivan had seen the man telephone.

In ten minutes Constable Olivan came through.

"Wait for me," said Mander. "I'll pick you up near the wall. And listen, Olivan; don't mention this to a soul—not to anybody in the division, or to any police officer you meet or may know...."

"Trust me, sir," said Olivan's reproachful voice.

* * * *

The taxicab that carried Inspector Mander of Scotland Yard to the rendezvous did not move fast enough for him. He jumped out, paying the driver at the corner of the street and, hurrying along, met Olivan.

"I thought I told you—" he began.

"Excuse me, sir," said the police officer, "In a case like this I've got to do me own thinking. I thought I'd have to have a consultation with you, and what's the good of doing it just outside his garden, where he might be hearing every word?"

The intelligence of this reply was rather staggering.

"Yes, of course."

Mander seldom admitted that he was wrong, but he did so now.

"Well, where is he?"

"In the factory, sir. He's made two journeys, and the last time, sir, I saw him take a gun out of his pocket and look at it before he put it back. It was an automatic, I'm sure, because I heard the jacket come back."

Now to do Mr. Mander every justice, he was not deficient in courage, and the fact that he might confront an armed Ringer did not in any way deter him, the more especially as he had also brought an automatic from his house in preparation for any such emergency, and he was a fairly good shot.

He gave his instructions in a low voice as they walked rapidly towards the passage.

"I'll go into the factory and you keep guard in the garden. You haven't got your police whistle?"

"Yes, I have sir," said Olivan proudly. "I brought that with me in case—"

"You're an extremely intelligent man, constable," said Mander graciously. "If you hear me shout blow your whistle—not before, you understand? When I've got him I don't mind who helps to put him inside. If there's any credit going for this job I want it myself."

"I think we ought to have it, too," said the constable.

If Mr. Mander noticed the "we," he did not contest the claims of his humble friend to recognition.

There was no sound in the garden when Mr. Mander was assisted over the wall. He went straight to the trapdoor, opened it, and flashed down the light of an electric lamp. There was a flight of stone steps, and down this he went, extinguishing the lamp before he moved into the vault-like passage which apparently ran under the factory.

He heard a queer sound: a distant whirr, a thud. Along he crept and turned into another passage which ran at right angles, not daring to use his lamp. And then, stretching out his hand to feel his way, he touched a human shoulder. Instantly he grappled with the unknown. The rough hair of a beard brushed his face as he gripped the intruder's throat.

"Go quietly," he shouted. "I've got you, and the house is surrounded by police!"

He heard the sound of running feet and then silence.

"I want you—"

Something hard and violent caught him under the jaw and he staggered back.

"I've got you covered; don't move!"

As he spoke he flashed the lamp upon the bearded man.

It was a very dishevelled Inspector Bliss.

* * * *

Next morning there was a discussion at the Yard.

"Naturally, the constable did not blow his whistle when he heard you shout," said Inspector Bliss with exaggerated politeness, "because the constable was Henry Arthur Milton, who had been playing you for the sucker that you are!

"Could you not choose some other time to make your dramatic appearance than the moment when I had located the printing works of the biggest gang of forgers that has ever operated in London? Happily, I had phoned

120

through to Scotland Yard for my reserves, and the most important of the gang were caught.

"Why do you imagine I spend my nights in an empty house if I hadn't some reason for it? It took me three months to locate that factory. It took you three minutes nearly to bust up three months' work! However, I'm bearing you no malice. The Ringer caught you, and that is my complete satisfaction."

As Mr. Mander walked towards the door Bliss called him back.

"You ought to write an article about this adventure of yours," he said offensively.

* * * * *

121

Chapter 13

The Accidental Snapshot

People have the most unlikely hobbies. Mrs. Gardling occupied her moments of leisure with photography. She had a small studio at the back of her house in Hampstead: it was one partitioned half of a garage that had been built to house four cars. Mrs. Gardling had only one car, though she could have afforded more.

Her favourite subjects were flowers, and she was dealing with some perfect Easter lilies in an exquisite Venetian vase that night when The Ringer, who was fleeing for his life, broke into her garage in his search for petrol.

He came out of complete darkness through the partition door into the blinding light of photographic lamps just as Mrs. Gardling was making an exposure. She saw him for a second before his hand closed over the switch and turned out the lights. But she saw him, as few people had ever done, without disguise.

As the lights went off he heard a drawer being pulled out and something hard scrape along the wood.

"Don't move or I'll shoot!" she said, and heard him laugh and the door slam behind him.

By the time the police came he had vanished. They told her they were pursuing a motorcar thief, but they did not tell her who that thief was because they were chary of talking about him and the newspapers getting to know that they had so nearly caught the man they were seeking.

So Mrs. Gardling cherished that photographic negative of Easter lilies rather as a curiosity than from its intrinsic value. Henry Arthur Milton, for his part, was quite unaware that this deadly thing was in the possession of a lady against whom he found it necessary at a later period to operate....

* * * *

The Ringer was in Berlin, a favourite haunt of his. Superintendent Bliss had a letter from him bearing a Charlottenburg postmark. The letter began, as usual, without formality:

> There is a lady with a club in Hogarth Street, Soho, on whom it
> might be worth your while to keep an eye. I thought of dealing with

her myself because her baseness (doesn't that word look queer?) had not brought her within the purview of the law. I think she might be very gently "moved on."

She dispenses drink in prohibited hours—a mild offence, but sufficient to put a check to her other activities. [Name: Mrs. Erita Gardling (born Demage). Address: The Red Monk Club, Hogarth Street. Previous conviction at Manchester, March 7, 1921, conspiracy to defraud. Six months second division.]

Henry Arthur Milton was an exasperating man, and nothing so distressed Mr. Bliss as this habit of putting the police under an obligation to him. He knew, before the wire he addressed to the Manchester police was answered, that The Ringer's data were exact.

The matter was handed to the divisional police, a raid was staged, and in due course Mrs. Gardling appeared before a police magistrate and was sent to prison with hard labour for three months.

Ordinarily this would have been a harsh sentence for selling liquor after hours, but the police found many things which were not described or even hinted at in The Ringer's letter. The amenities of the club were apparently much more extensive than desirable.

Who it was that had betrayed the fact that the raid was made at the instigation of the notorious criminal, Bliss found it difficult to discover. He was a stickler for official secrecy, and it is no exaggeration to say that when Mrs. Gardling turned round as she was leaving the dock and said, in a voice vehement with fury: "You can tell your friend The Ringer that he'll be sorry he ever interfered with me," Bliss was furious.

The divisional inspector denied that he had revealed the part The Ringer had played; the other detectives in the raid were equally emphatic, though it was one of these who had light-heartedly taunted Mrs. Gardling with the name of the informant.

Mrs. Gardling was a rich woman who had afforded to marry her daughter into respectable society. How madam obtained her wealth was no mystery. She ran profitable side-lines to the club business, and many a cheque for a large amount had gone into her bank as the price of her silence about certain disreputable happenings to which she was privy.

When she was waiting to be removed to Holloway she saw the detective who had given her the identity of the informer, and he was rather agitated because his chief had had an unpleasant interview with Bliss and had passed the kick down.

"For the Lord's sake, Mrs. Gardling, don't mention the fact to anybody that it was I who told you The Ringer squeaked on you."

She, who should have been wilting in shame, was boiling with anger.

"I'd like to know that fellow!" she said, incoherent in her justifiable annoyance. "I'd spend ten thousand pounds to get him! Oh, yes, of course I've heard of him, you fool—who hasn't?"

"It's a curious thing," said the loquacious officer of the law, "that the only time I ever met you before, Mrs. Gardling, was the night he broke into your house and pinched petrol—"

She stared at him.

"The Ringer? Was that man The Ringer?" she gasped. "Your people said it was a burglar—"

"Car thief," he corrected, rather satisfied with the sensation he had created. "Yes, that was The Ringer. It's a regular coincidence! He busts your house and now he's bust you!"

But Mrs. Gardling wasn't thinking of coincidences.

She had permission to see her well-married daughter before the removal to Holloway.

"Annie," she said, "go up to 'The Linnets' and in the studio you'll find a black tin box full of negatives. Take it to the bank and ask the manager to keep it locked up till I come out."

"Aren't you going to appeal, mamma?" asked her daughter.

"I'll be out quicker by saying nothing," she said. "And get the lease of that house in Maddox Street; we can wangle a licence for it—we'll call it 'The Furnace Club.' I thought that out last night."

* * * *

So passed to a prison laundry in North London the famous Mrs. Gardling, and her mind during the period of her incarceration was equally divided between plans for her new club and methods by which she could bring to justice the man she loathed.

It was unfortunate to some extent that Annie, her daughter, desired most passionately to assist her mother in her material rehabilitation. The well-married one was a bright girl, brisk and businesslike, and too well she knew the power of the Press. Her mother had been absent for a month when she sent out a little helpful propaganda for the Furnace Club.

She was not a particularly clever writer, but, as some of us know, it is not necessary to be clever to be interesting, and the news editor of the *Weekly Post-Herald*, scanning the typewritten effusions she sent to him, and scanning them with an apathetic eye, came upon a paragraph which quickened his interest. He rang a bell and sent for a reporter.

"Call on this woman and see what there is in the story." He blue-pencilled the paragraph.

During the following week there appeared an interesting column. "The Ringer's Vengeance," it was headed, a little hectically, and it told the story of the midnight visit, when Mrs. Gardling was photographing flowers.

"My mother has often spoken to me of the man's face which had appeared on the negative, but because she has always had a sympathetic heart towards the unfortunate she never brought this picture to the notice of the police.

"I have no doubt at all that The Ringer concocted these stories about my mother, who is perfectly innocent of all the dreadful things which have been said about her...."

In the course of the article it was stated that the interesting negative was in a safe place and that "more would be heard of it."

Curiously enough, Bliss did not give the article a great deal of attention, and the only thing which really interested him was the revelation that the Furnace Club was to be opened in the near future under the care and management of the well-married daughter.

As for this lady, she realised that she had said a great deal too much and refused all further interviews, quaking a little as to what would be the effect upon her fond mother when that resolute woman came out of prison.

She could hardly consult her husband on the matter, for Mr. Leppold, that dark, handsome man, was not on speaking terms with his mother-in-law, and whenever her name obtruded into the conversation he invariably excised it.

"Don't talk to me about that old so-and-so," was his favourite expression.

Ann Leppold bridled but was silent. Mrs. Gardling had been very rude to Alfred, though undoubtedly her exasperation had cause. He had first appeared at the club as Count Giolini. He wasn't a count at all—this fact was not discovered until after the marriage.

In other respects she had little to complain of; he was a well-off man, had a beautiful flat off Jermyn Street, lived expensively, presented jewels to his wife, and took her away every year to Monte Carlo, Deauville, and other fashionable resorts.

She often wondered what his business was, for, although he claimed to be something in the City, he had no office, and spent most of his time in the West End of London. Whatever it was, it did not keep him very busy. He was never away for more than a few days at a time, and, generally speaking, his life was quiet and inoffensive.

She spoke to him about The Ringer but he was rather uninterested. Most of the evenings at home he spent reading the newspapers, the City pages being of special significance, for he was a frugal man who had invested well and hoped some day to retire and live in Paris, a city for which he had a great affection, though he seldom went there.

She was an avid reader of newspapers herself, but confined her studies to those fascinating episodes which are revealed in the courts of law.

One night—it was about a week before her mother was sent to prison—she laid the paper down on her knees.

"It's perfectly awful the way these robberies are going on, Alf," she said. "One of these gangs took over forty thousand pounds' worth of diamonds from a place in Hatton Garden on Sunday, and got away without leaving a trace. I think the police must be in it. Now, if I were the police—"

"You're not," snapped her husband from behind his newspaper; "and the best thing you can do is to shut up."

Annie closed her lips firmly. When she had been married somebody had given her a book entitled "How to be Happy though Married," and she had learned the lesson of bearing and forbearing.

At Scotland Yard they accepted this succession of burglaries with philosophic calm. The police were only human, and if shop-owners refused to take elementary precautions, such as employing watchmen, buying safes which offered six hours' resistance to the best of burglars, that was their look-out.

The police did all they possibly could, and followed a routine which is usually very effective. But Scotland Yard had neither second sight nor the power of divination.

"It might be Lewing or Martin or Crooford," speculated Mr. Bliss, "or it may be that Paris gang that come over specially for these jobs."

The gangs which operate from foreign cities are the most difficult to trace. Paris is seven hours from London, and, supposing that one of the gang were in London, making all the preliminary investigations, completing the time-table, and getting together the necessary apparatus and tools, they could arrive on Saturday evening, and leave on Monday morning with the bulk of their loot.

"The thing to do is to find the caretaker," said Bliss.

By this he referred to the one member of the gang permanently established in London.

* * * *

Mr. Leppold did not even read the interview with his wife in the *Weekly Post-Herald*, he merely saw her name in a column of print and admonished her.

"The advice I give to you, my girl, is to keep out of the public eye. There's no reason why you should go shoving yourself forward into the limelight."

"I am doing something for my poor, dear mother," said Mrs. Leppold hotly, "and I've a good mind to get that box out of the Northern and Southern—"

Mr. Leppold became instantly interested.

"Does your mother bank at the Northern and Southern?"

"She has for years," said Annie complacently, because the Northern and Southern is rather an exclusive banking company.

"She keeps all her papers—what are you laughing at?"

"I wasn't laughing," said Alf Leppold as he took up his newspaper again; but she gathered, from the fact that the sheet shook convulsively, that he was lying.

"What's the joke?" she demanded.

"Something I read in the paper," was his reply.

After she had gone to bed he went into his study and put through a call to Paris. For six minutes he spoke cryptically. He often spoke over the Paris wire, and he always spoke cryptically.

The next day he went to the south of London and had tea with a bearded Army pensioner who was a widower and lived alone in two rooms in a model dwelling, and had a grievance against society, particularly that eminent section of society represented by the Stewards of the Jockey Club.

"They ought to warn off...."

He named a number of eminent trainers whose horses had not won that afternoon at Hurst Park. This bearded man backed horses on a system, though his employers would have dropped in their tracks if they had even suspected his favourite recreation. If he had not backed horses, Mr. Leppold would never have got to know him.

He soothed the disgruntled punter with certain alluring prospects.

"You stay on for a month, then off you pop to South America or South Africa or anywhere you like. There's five thousand pounds—more than you'd earn in fifty years—"

"I should lose my pension," said the man, looking at him from under his beetling black brows. "And what about my good name?"

"You'll lose that anyway," said Mr. Leppold coolly. "The first time your boss knows that you owe money to bookmakers your name will be mud. I'm paying you five hundred pounds on account," he went on, counting out the notes. "I trust you, and you've got to trust me. I'll knock twice on the side door, like this." He sounded a morse B on the table. "All you've got to do is to let us in."

The man moved uncomfortably.

"What about tying me up?" he suggested.

"You needn't worry about that," said Mr. Leppold, secretly amused. "We'll stick an alibi on to you that you couldn't blow off with dynamite."

The man gathered up the money, and after Mr. Leppold had left put it in a safe place. He thought the scheme was a very simple one, that detection was impossible. The prisons of Great Britain and the United States are filled with men who have harboured similar illusions.

* * * *

When Mr. Leppold got home that night he found his wife a preening piece of self-importance.

"I've had a letter from dear mother," she said, "about that Ringer."

For once he did not silence her.

"What about that Ringer?" he demanded.

"It's his photograph that mother took. I've been talking on the phone to Scotland Yard." (Mr. Leppold blinked, but said nothing.) "A gentleman named Bliss said it's most important, and I'm to get the photograph tomorrow and take it to him. It appears they haven't got a picture of this fellow, and I might get the thousand pounds reward."

"Good luck to you, my girl!" said Mr. Leppold heartily. "That fellow ought to be hung—he double-crossed a friend of mine." He did not particularise the friend or the circumstances.

He was in a very cheerful mood throughout the dinner, of which he partook sparingly, for one thinks most quickly on an empty stomach. After the meal was over he went to the study, locked the door, and took from a safe a small leather packet of tools and put it into his overcoat pocket.

He could afford to be cheerful, for he was embarking upon one of the easiest jobs he had ever undertaken.

At half-past ten o'clock he arrived at a bar near Shaftesbury Avenue, and saw, without any apparent recognition, the two men who had arrived from Paris that night. Ten minutes later he walked out of the saloon and the two men followed him. At a convenient place he stopped to light a cigar, and they came up with him.

"The thing's sweet," he said. "There's enough foreign currency in the vault to make it worth while—about seven thousand pounds in Treasury notes and eighteen thousand in bank-notes."

"Is it a dead shop?" asked one.

"No," said Mr. Leppold, "it's live. The assistant manager lives over, but he's gone into the country to see his mother, who's ill."

How Mr. Leppold obtained all these details is entirely his own business.

He walked down a side street, tapped at the private door of the bank, and it was opened instantly. He was hardly inside before the other two joined him. The door was locked.

"What about this tying up?" asked Mr. Leppold of the bearded man, but the watchman showed no inclination to submit to any tying.

"You can tie me before you go," he urged. "I'd like to see how you do the job."

Leppold, who was a man of few words, nodded. He had no need of a guide; he opened the steel grille leading to the vault and went down the stone steps, followed by three men; the key of that grille was the one duplicate he possessed.

At the end of a short passage was another grille. Workmen had been here, and great oblong cavities had been chiselled in the stone. "They're putting a real safe door on," explained Mr. Leppold, and added: "About time!"

The bearded watchman gaped at the three experts as they attacked the lock. In an hour it was removed and the heavy steel-barred door swung open. A light burned in the arched roof and showed the contents of the vault. Stacked in three lines were a number of deed boxes, and at the sight of these Mr. Leppold, who had a grim sense of humour, chuckled.

"Half a minute," he said.

He walked quickly along till he came to a deed box, and this he tapped with his knuckle.

"Ma's," he said sardonically.

It bore the initials "S. A. G.," Mrs. Gardling's Christian names being Sarah Ann.

"My missus is going to get a thing out of there tomorrow that'll do The Ringer a bit of no good."

"What about this money?" said one of his companions impatiently, and for half an hour they were working industriously, collecting and sorting.

* * * *

The three men wore overcoats and each overcoat was cunningly pocketed. They were swift workers all, and the money was disposed of almost as soon as it was brought into view.

"Now I think we'd better tie up whiskers," said Leppold, and produced a rope from his pocket.

They looked around, but the bearded man was not in the room. They saw him, however, on the other side of the grille; he had a black box, which was open, and at the moment they came in sight of him he had produced a dark-looking negative and was holding it up to the light.

"Who locked this gate?" demanded Mr. Leppold.

The watchman looked round.

"I did," he said calmly. "You left the key in the lock, which was rather foolish."

"Well, unlock it, quick!" He was carrying in his hand the small kit of tools with which they had forced the downstairs lock.

Suddenly the watchman's arm shot through the grating, and there was an automatic attached to it. The muzzle pressed against Mr. Leppold's stomach.

"Hand over those tools!"

The dazed man obeyed.

"And if any of you pull a gun," said the 'watchman' calmly, "you'll know less about the cause of your death than the coroner who sits on you."

"Who the hell are you?" asked Leppold.

"My name is Henry Arthur Milton, vulgarly called The Ringer," said the other. "And, by the way, if you want the real night watchman you'll find him tied up in the manager's office—really tied up. And the least you can do is to tell the police that you did the tying.

"I've been trailing that ancient sinner for a few days; I was, in fact, in his bedroom when you were discussing tonight's little adventure. He was a little surprised when he got the signal on the side door an hour too soon."

He folded the negative and carefully put it in his pocket.

"Give my love to mamma," he said, as he moved out of view and out of range.

Mr. Leppold never forgave him that, and even in the morning, when the police arrived, he was still brooding upon the insult.

Chapter 14

The Sinister Dr. Lutteur

Inspector Mander had a great friend—at least, Miss Carberry was not as great a friend as he could have wished her to be.

He thought Scotland Yard was the most interesting place in the world and talked about it all the time. She had a weakness for musical comedy and the more respectable kind of night clubs, where the orangeade sold after licensed hours really is orangeade. When he talked of crime she was bored. When she told him of the perfectly marvellous dance records that had recently been issued he tried to bring the subject back to crime.

She frequently met a distinguished stranger, who would have taken her to musical comedies and night clubs, but was afraid he would get her a bad name, so they dined at nice little restaurants instead. She called him Ernest, which was not his name, though she was unaware of the fact. As to her apathy in the matter of Scotland Yard's activities, she was not to be blamed.

There is nothing romantic about crime. To be a successful detective does not require a super-intelligence, but the power of reducing your mind to the lowest possible level of intelligence. The great detectives are those who are able to lower their mentality to the level of the men whose ill-work they are endeavouring to counteract.

This was the thesis of an impromptu lecture which Superintendent Bliss delivered to his crestfallen subordinate.

"The trouble with you, Mander," he said, "is that you try to be clever. Instead of being your natural self and establishing contact with the normal criminal mind you waste the time you should devote to sleeping in working out theories based, as far as I can gather, upon those sensational detective novels which were so popular twenty years ago. I have a feeling that you are writing a monograph on cigar ash."

Mr. Mander writhed under the accusation.

"A criminal of the type I am looking for," Bliss continued remorselessly, "does not wear evening dress or frequent the more fashionable restaurants of the West End. You are more likely to find him in a public-house near the Elephant and Castle, and there is no need for you to employ logic or deduction. All you have to be is a good listener, for Libby is the type of man who makes a serial story of his adventures."

"I wasn't exactly looking for Libby," said Mr. Mander, stung to defence. "I had a theory about The Ringer—"

Superintendent Bliss groaned.

"Libby is a common and a cheap maker of counterfeit coins," he said. "He is a sordid, ten-conviction criminal. If you are under the impression that The Ringer has the slightest association with that type of individual you are greatly mistaken."

But here Mr. Bliss was to some extent wrong.

The incidence of the underworld, the real cheap, hard-labour men, never failed to interest Henry Arthur Milton. His view of the lower strata of law-breakers was no more flattering than were those of Superintendent Bliss; but, as it happened, he was at that moment especially absorbed in the career of quite a number of very poor people, most of whom gained their livelihood by illicit means.

* * * *

The Ringer was lodging at a house in Enther Street, Lambeth—rather larger than the ordinary type of poor house—a place kept scrupulously clean, where the scrubbing brush sounded most of the day. His landlady was Mrs. Kilford, a widow. She had two daughters, one of whom, Nelly, was both pretty and curious. The prettiness he recognised; her curiosity he discovered when she went up to his room one morning with a cup of un-palatable tea and lingered at the door to discuss her affairs.

"…Of course, he's much older than me, but quite refined. Mother says he ought to come to the house, but he won't. He's terribly shy."

"Blushing lad," said Henry Arthur Milton, who was in a cheerful mood.

He had no particular business in London at the moment except to avoid the attentions of people who wished to see him very badly. He was certainly not passionately interested in the love affairs of his landlady's daughter. More exhilarating was the knowledge that right opposite him lived one called Libby, who was a maker of counterfeit coins; for The Ringer had an especial grudge against manufacturers of half-crowns, who rob little trades-men and other people to whom half a crown is quite an enormous sum of money.

He was returning home rather late one night when he saw Nelly at the corner of the mean street in which he lived. She was talking to a man who was a head taller than she and who, when he came abreast, turned his face so that Henry Arthur Milton could not see it very distinctly. As he passed he heard Nelly say: "But I have never been a lady's maid."

He expected her the next morning to offer her confidence, but she was remarkably silent. A week later her mother told him tearfully that Nelly had run away and married Mr. Hackitt. The only consolation so far as The Ringer could gather was that the marriage had been most properly performed at a registrar's office and a copy of the marriage certificate had been forwarded to the landlady.

More amazingly, the bride announced that she and her husband were going to Paris for their honeymoon.

"Which is in France," explained the landlady unnecessarily.

* * * *

The Ringer could not spare a corner of his mind to be occupied by Nelly's love affair. He dismissed the matter and devoted his entire attention to the undoing of Libby.

He himself never attempted to usurp the functions of the law. If a criminal committed an offence for which the law could punish him he was satisfied that the machinery of Scotland Yard should be put in motion.

One night, on information received, the Flying Squad descended on Mr. Libby and removed him with a hundredweight of metal, a number of excellent dies and electro-plating apparatus, and when the affair was cleared up Superintendent Bliss decided to comb the neighbourhood for the informant, who, he knew, was The Ringer. But that gentleman had anticipated some such move and had disappeared.

It was in the Strand between eleven and twelve one night when the theatre crowds were turning out and the roadway was a confusion of cars, taxicabs, and omnibuses that he saw and recognised Nelly's mysterious lover. There was no need to see his face; The Ringer remembered people by their backs, their walk, the movement of their hands, and he was as well satisfied that this man was Hackitt as though he were identifying him from a studio portrait.

Mr. Hackitt had no right to be in London; he should have been in Paris on his honeymoon. He certainly had no right whatever to be wearing a top hat and a coat obviously made by a good tailor. He was alone, moving in the leisured manner of one who was walking by preference. And by his side was a lady who was not Nelly.

Since it was the business of The Ringer to know the affairs of his enemies, he recognised the lady as a Miss Carberry, who was friendly with Inspector Mander. If she had not been "attached" to Inspector Mander he would not have known her at all.

"But how perfectly fascinating!" said The Ringer.

* * * *

It was a few days after this that the centre of his interest changed to Esher.

The nursing home of Doctor Lutteur in that village was a beautiful if modest house situated in ample grounds, and if the doctor's clientele was not large it was exclusive. He was an extremely agreeable gentleman, who went out of his way to make his clients comfortable and happy, and there were few establishments which could equal it in point of comfort and up-to-date equipment. He was a fairly wealthy man, unmarried, had no hobbies but his work, and was beloved by his patients and the few people who were admitted into the limited circle of friendship.

He could afford to pick and choose his patients, and if he showed a preference for those who promised to give him the least trouble he could hardly be blamed.

Mr. Roos, his new patient, was hardly the kind he would have chosen, for Mr. Roos was rather hearty, not to say boastful—a noisy man, and the doctor disliked noisy men.

"An aunt of mine came to you, doctor, about four or five years ago. She wrote out to me in South Africa and said you'd looked after her better than any other doctor she'd ever had, and you're the man for my money!"

He had had a nervous breakdown on the ship; in fact his condition was such that he was nearly landed at Madeira, he said.

"Cash is no object to me. I can promise you this—that if you take me in you're not going to be bothered with visitors, because I don't know anybody in this damned country and don't want to!"

He exhibited certain signs of nervousness; his hands shook, his face twitched at odd intervals; the shrewd Dr. Lutteur diagnosed the case as the after-effects of heavy drinking. But he did not like noisy people, or hearty people, or people who talked loudly of their vast possessions.

Nevertheless, he gave a bed and a room to his new patient, prescribed a diet, and was agreeably surprised to discover that Mr. Roos was content to lie in bed and read newspapers and showed no inclination to disturb his other patients.

There were three, the most interesting of whom was an elderly lady who had been under his care for two years. Mr. Roos saw her once in the garden being wheeled about in a bath-chair, a pale, severe woman who regarded him with the greatest suspicion. A surly gardener, who had been rude to her for picking his spring flowers and had been given a week's notice by the doctor, said her name was Timms—Miss Alicia Timms.

Roos had been there the greater part of the week when a visitor called. It was the afternoon, when the patients were resting in various parts of the grounds, and when Mr. Roos found it rather difficult to prevent himself from falling asleep, for the weather was warm, the silence, the fragrance of the fresh spring air, all things combined to induce that pleasant state of coma which attends a good luncheon.

The doctor's study was under his bedroom, and the shrill voice of the woman pierced with startling distinctness the quiet of the house. He heard her angry protestations, heard the doctor's frantic request for silence, and then the voices sank to an indistinguishable rumble of sound, which only occasionally rose to audibility.

Mr. Roos had risen that day and was lying fully dressed upon his bed. He gathered up his book and his spectacles and went into the grounds, whence he saw the station fly carrying the visitor down the drive towards the main road. Dr. Lutteur's three prize patients were dozing; the disgruntled gardener was very wide awake.

"I shan't be sorry to leave here, anyway," he said. "You never see anybody but a lot of old people, and you don't see them long before one of 'em pops off! We've only had one patient here that didn't peg out."

"Thank you, my cheery soul," said Mr. Roos.

But the gardener insisted, with a certain gloomy satisfaction, on the high mortality of patients at Dr. Lutteur's house.

"Naturally, they die because they're old. I suppose he's a pretty good doctor but you can't make old people young, can you? The only one that didn't die here was an old gentleman who was taken away by his relations. And they know they're going to die—they're always making their wills.

"That old lady over there, Miss Timms—she's worth pots of money! Mind you, I respect her; she's left every penny to a lady's maid who used to look after her. I know because I witnessed the will and I had a good look at it because the old lady had a sort of fainting fit after she'd signed."

"Do you remember the name of the lady's maid?" asked Mr. Roos, carelessly.

The gardener looked up at the sky for inspiration.

"Yes, Hachett or Hackitt, or some such name. The last old lady that died here left all her money to a woman called—I forget her name; the only thing I do remember about her is that she fell in the river and was drowned about six months after she'd drawn the money. And then there was an old gentleman named—I don't remember his name—who left fifty thousand pounds to a girl whose father he knew when he was a boy.

"I was telling this to the young lady who came down here yesterday when the doctor was at Bagshot; a nice-looking girl she was, very much like that young lady who came in the cab to see the doctor about an hour ago."

Late that night, when the patients were asleep, or should have been asleep, the girl who had called earlier in the day came to the house. Mr. Roos, lying full length on the floor, with a small microphone fixed to his

135

ear, listened with the greatest interest to the more or less confused conversation.

"…Well, I may be curious, but I've found *you* out!… followed you to Waterloo Station…. What is the meaning of it?…"

Later she became less truculent, agreed to something or other. Mr. Roos heard the words "little house."

He could not have heard it all, because when he learned, two or three days later, that the doctor was called away on business to Paris and had left a locum tenens to look after the inmates of the home he was taken by surprise.

The patient left the nursing home within an hour of receiving this information; but it took a long time for him to locate the doctor.

The quietness of Enther Street, Lambeth, was disturbed by a loud scream. The hour was 2 a.m. and in this drab neighbourhood a midnight scream was not an unusual phenomenon. At the corner of the street two policemen had met at the limit of their respective beats, and they were, contrary to regulations, smoking. One turned his head in the direction of the sound and remarked casually that somebody was "getting a lacing." They waited expectantly for the second and the successive cries, but they did not come.

Now a succession of such screams is normal. One shrill cry of horror that has no companion has a sinister significance. The two officers walked slowly down the street. They saw a window open and a tousled head stuck out.

"Next door," said the owner of the head—a man. "That's the first noise the new people have made since they've been here. Half a tick. I'll come down."

These police officers were not unused to the ways of the officious informant: they were rather amused. The man came out from his front door wearing an overcoat.

"There's a man and a woman live there; they moved in last Monday. Nobody's seen either of 'em. My missus, though, saw 'em move in—brought their furniture in a motor-van one night when it was raining. Nobody's ever seen 'em go out."

One of the police looked up at the mean face of the house. It consisted of two floors, the ground and the upper. A tall man with a fishing rod could reach the guttering of the slate roof. There were two windows above, a door and a window below—the kind of brick box you can have for a few shillings a week.

"Well," said the officer of the law, with the profundity of his kind, "you can't do anything to people because they don't come out of their houses."

136

The neighbour agreed, and there the party might have dispersed, the policemen to their interrupted smoke, the householder to his bed, only the second policeman saw a light in the upper window. It flickered up and down, grew to a yellow brightness, and sank to a dull red.

"That room's on fire!" he said, and whipped out his truncheon.

The hammering on the door awakened the street. A panel smashed and a gloved hand went in, groping for the lock. As the door was flung open a great cloud of smoke rolled forth.

"Get the people out of the other houses, Harry!" spluttered the officer. "Mr. What's-your-name, run to the fire alarm at the corner."

He blundered into the house, felt his way up the stairs and threw open the door of the front room. The heat of the blazing floor drove him back, but he saw the woman lying half on and half off the smouldering bed. Bracing one foot upon a burning rafter, he reached out and dragged her through the flames.

It was a superhuman task to carry the weight down those narrow stairs that sagged under him. He blundered once on the landing and nearly fell. Presently he staggered out into the open. The fire engines arrived at that moment. The ambulance arrived a few minutes later, and they laid the woman on a stretcher and rushed her to the nearest hospital.

She was still living, in spite of the knife wound in her side, but died after admission. She was young and rather pretty.

The policeman telephoned to his superior and went back to pursue his inquiries, the affair having occurred on his beat.

Inspector Mander reported to his chief the following morning.

"It's a very ordinary case. A man named Brown knifed his wife, and in the struggle the lamp must have overturned. We haven't got Brown yet, but I've circulated his description."

Bliss had read the official report furnished by the divisional inspector.

"Apart from the fact that nobody knows that his name is Brown, and nobody has ever seen him, and that the floor was sprinkled with petrol, and that the house was deliberately set on fire, your account and prognostications seem fairly accurate. The case had better go to Lindon. It is in his area."

All day long detectives and firemen searched amid the blackened debris for the missing man. But he was some distance away and very much alive.

Dr. Lutteur sat in his study, a medical work propped up on the table before him, a long cigar between his even white teeth. He closed the book, put it away on a shelf, and drew from a drawer of his desk a sheet of foolscap paper. He read this carefully, then he rang the bell. A nursing sister answered it within a few minutes.

"Oh, sister, about Miss Timms; she's been bothering me all day about making a new will."

"She only made one a month or so ago," said the nursing sister. "Didn't she leave all her money to a woman called Hackitt?"

The doctor nodded.

"Apparently she's changed her mind," he said. "She wishes now to leave it to the daughter of an old friend of hers, a Miss Carberry. I've got the name in the will." He pointed to the document. "Will you come along and witness it?"

The nursing sister looked dubious.

"She doesn't seem to be in a condition to make a will. Do you think it's wise—" she began.

"It amuses her. She'll probably change her mind again in the course of a few days," said the doctor calmly. "Let us go up and get her signature while she's still awake. The night sister can witness it as well as you."

The clock was striking one; the doctor had locked away the new will in his safe, had risen and was preparing for bed when a perfect stranger rang the bell of the nursing home. He had come in a car and had three companions. Lutteur looked at the bearded face and wondered where he had seen it before.

"My name is Superintendent Bliss, of Scotland Yard," said the caller in cold and even tones. "I am inquiring into the death of a woman called Brown, who was murdered in Enther Street, Lambeth. I am also inquiring into the death of two other women who were legatees of estates left by former patients of yours. I shall ask you to accompany me to the Kingston Police Station."

It was all very formal and meaningless. Weeks after, when Dr. Lutteur was awaiting execution, he could not quite understand what had happened.

* * * *

"Lutteur's system," explained Mr. Bliss to Inspector Mander, "was a very simple one. He ran a nursing home, and there is no suggestion that any of the patients who died in his charge were the victims of foul play. They died natural deaths, but he chose his patients rather well. He scoured the country, looking for wealthy women without any near relations.

"By some means he persuaded them to go into his home—we found the most marvellous collection of literature, with expensive photographs of the grounds and the treatment rooms—and, once there, the rest was a fairly simple matter.

"He first of all chose the legatee. Then, either by the administration of a drug which destroyed their will power or by his personal magnetism he induced them to make a will in favour of his nominee. Whether he married the nominee in every case I do not know. He certainly married Mrs. Kilford's daughter and killed her when he discovered that she knew who he was. He would have done the same with the girl Carberry—"

"Carberry?" said Mander. "I know a girl called Carberry. By the way, how did you get on to this story, chief?"

"Information received," said Bliss diplomatically. "And don't call me chief!"

Chapter 15

The Obliging Cobbler

Doctors are credited with an aversion for their own medicines. It was because of this aversion that Henry Arthur Milton found himself with two feuds on his hands. The first of these was with two brothers named Pelcher. They were specialists, but nobody referred to them by that title. The police called them "The Two"; damaged householders found descriptions which varied in their vitriolic quality according to their wealth of vocabulary.

Marlow Joyner, the latest of their victims, lay in bed with his head heavily bandaged, and told, haltingly and painfully, the story of his experience to a select audience consisting of a London police magistrate, Superintendent Bliss, and two police stenographers.

For Mr. Marlow Joyner was on the danger list, and the doctors said that it was going to be a toss-up whether he ever left his bed alive. Happily, as it proved, the doctors were wrong, but it was touch and go for a week.

Bliss took the deposition back to Scotland Yard.

"I don't know which I'd rather take, The Two or The Ringer, but I know which would be the greatest loss to society."

"Maybe The Two is The Ringer?" suggested Inspector Mander hopefully.

Bliss turned his cold eyes upon the fatuous man.

"The Ringer has adopted many disguises," he said, "but I cannot remember that he has ever appeared at one and the same time as two people—except to the hopelessly intoxicated."

In a sense, the Superintendent was right, in a sense, wrong. There was an occasion when The Ringer was three men, but, as the greatest of tale-tellers has said, "that is another story."

* * * *

What was a secret to Scotland Yard was no secret to The Ringer, who, through his peculiarly effective organisation, was able to bring home to these two respectable young men—they lived in the suburbs and in their spare time cultivated roses—responsibility for their many acts.

For five weeks he sought evidence which would convince a police magistrate, but this was difficult to come by, and in the end he decided that this was a matter for "private treatment."

In the early hours of the morning the two brothers were picked up in the street in which they lived and rushed to the hospital.

They were as terribly bludgeoned as any of their victims had been, and it was eight weeks before the first of them was convalescent. They gave no information to the police except that they had been attacked by "a gang of roughs." Neither told the story of the solitary man who accosted them late one night.

"You've heard of me—I am The Ringer, and I'm rather annoyed with you two thugs...."

While they had been debating how best to deal with the man—naturally, they were disinclined to make trouble so close to their own home—something hit the nearest. It might have been a rubber truncheon; the victim wasn't sure. His brother, who rushed to the rescue, had no doubt at all that it was something effective. The blow that caught him did not stun him, but knocked him out. When he awoke he was in the one bed and his brother was in the next.

They were released from hospital at last and reached, spontaneously, a common agreement.

"From what you know and I know, Harry," said one, "we ought to get this bird."

* * * *

The second feud was developed more violently, in a fashionable Viennese café, when "Kelly" Rosefield missed the man he hated with his first shot. The strange man in the black wideawake hat fired the second, and Kelly went down with a bullet in the bony part of his shoulder. The curious thing about it was that the successful marksman was entirely in the right.

Kelly used to beat up his woman partner when he felt that way. They lived in an expensive block of flats; the interfering gentleman who stole in upon them one night—Kelly had most carelessly left the flat door open—lived in the apartment beneath. What he did to the wife-beater was a subject for comment, commiseration, and explanation among Mr. Rosefield's friends for many a day.

Kelly explained his injuries variously. He had been knocked over by a car, he had fallen against a lamp standard, he had been thrown when riding a spirited blood horse. And in all these prevarications he was assisted by the woman called Carmenflora, who had most reason to gloat over his enlarged countenance.

Carmenflora was more bitter than her man; and when the matter ended as it did, and Kelly was lying in hospital—nobody quite certain as to the brand of spiritual consolation appropriate to his condition—Carmenflora went forth and looked for the interfering gentleman.

But Henry Arthur Milton knew that other people were looking for him. You cannot shoot off automatics in Viennese restaurants, fashionable or unfashionable, without inviting the attention of the local constabulary. He faded to Berlin.

Four months later he was entering his London hotel and came face to face with Carmenflora, who recognised him. She said nothing, but he caught the flicker of her eyes, read their story, and, going up to his room, packed his handbag, phoned for his bill, and was out of the hotel in half an hour.

Therefore there were three people looking for The Ringer—or 18,004, if the active and intelligent members of the Metropolitan Police Force be included.

* * * *

There were people who called The Ringer clever. He never laid claim to any such title. He was painstaking, thorough, left nothing to chance, examined his ground with the finicky care of a very conscientious staff officer.

He did not believe in luck, good or bad, and found no excuse for such failures as he had. He had his vanities, but they were of a harmless sort, judged by the meaner ones common to humanity.

"I'll get that feller if I have to wait fifty-five years," said Kelly extravagantly.

Now Kelly was, by the Scotland Yard standard, a pretty bad man. He was a thief and an associate of thieves, and, with the assistance of his partner, who was courteously described as his wife, he had cleaned up considerable sums of money, mainly from susceptible young men, for Carmenflora was pretty and could be very, very attractive.

Bliss heard of his arrival and sent a polite sergeant to inquire if he was staying long in London.

"I'm a British subject and you can't deport me," said Kelly hotly. "I'm here on private business."

"We can't deport you further than Wormwood Scrubs," said the police sergeant gently, "but that's one of the foreign countries you'd hate to visit, Kelly. And that's just where you'll be if I find you giving nice little supper parties to young gentlemen."

Kelly winced at that, for the previous night he had entertained the impecunious son of a millionaire. Most millionaires' sons are impecunious, but their fathers will pay almost anything to keep the family name out of the newspapers. But this was the merest sideline.

"If it hurts you to see somebody else getting a free drink—" he began.

The polite sergeant became impolite very suddenly.

"Let's fan you for that old gun of yours," he said, and Kelly submitted to the outrage. As he could afford to do, for his automatic was well hidden.

When the visit was reported to Bliss the superintendent was rather interested.

"I've just had a report through from the Austrian police," he said. "Kelly's been shot up by somebody and Blunthall advances a theory that the somebody was The Ringer. If that is so The Ringer is in London."

He sent for Mander, who had his uses.

"I have an idea that we may get a line to The Ringer through Kelly," he said. "And there's another little matter which I'd like you to clear up. You remember the two brothers Pelcher, who were admitted to the Lewisham Hospital pretty well beaten up about six months ago?"

Mander remembered.

"I want them kept under observation. I don't say they are The Two, but the information I have from the divisional inspector has made me a little suspicious. If they are The Two then that is The Ringer's work also."

"They seem fairly respectable men: they are both working in the City—" began Mander.

"That doesn't make them respectable," said the superintendent.

* * * *

Kelly was a wealthy man. He could afford to live in the best hotel; he could afford to employ private detectives in his search for the man he loathed. He could also have afforded to have given his "wife" and partner complete control of her jewellery; but, like so many of his kind, he was mean to an extraordinary degree. For example, in all their Continental journeyings his wife invariably travelled second-class, while he lorded it in superior accommodation.

But his chief eccentricity was in relation to the jewels. His vanity demanded that his lady should appear beautifully and, indeed, extravagantly bedecked. Her necklace, her diamond bracelet, her rings and brooches he carried in a long case which fitted into his hip pocket. Every evening before dinner the jewels were given to her; every night, on her retirement, they were taken away and safely stored in the case.

There was an excellent reason for this. A previous partner, who had slaved for him and whom he had misguidedly trusted with jewellery, had disappeared, carrying with her about two thousand pounds' worth of portable property.

He was "serving out" the evening allowance of adornment when the floor-waiter knocked at his door and told him there was a man who wished to see him. Kelly, whose mind ran to detectives, asked for a description, and was relieved to learn that the caller was an elderly gentleman.

"Gentleman" was perhaps an exaggeration; he was obviously a working man; he confessed to being a cobbler—a mender of old shoes—a grey-haired man, shabbily attired, who wore spectacles and a bristling, iron-grey moustache. He was obviously nervous, and would not speak until the partner had been peremptorily ordered into the next room.

"It's about a lodger of mine, sir," said the cobbler nervously. "I don't want to interfere with anything I ought not to interfere in. I've lived in the same house for twenty-five years and I've never owed anybody a shilling, let alone got myself mixed up in any scandal. This lodger of mine...."

The lodger had been staying with him three weeks—a quiet man, who only went out in the evenings—a perfectly natural thing to do, since he was, as he said, a night watchman.

"But I've had my suspicions of him," said the cobbler-landlord, who gave his name as Hays; "and the other night, after he went out, I opened his bedroom door with one of my keys and I found the table covered with plans of this hotel."

"I didn't know it was this hotel," he went on, "but it happens to be the only hotel in the street."

"Plans?"

* * * *

The cobbler felt in his pocket, produced a transparent sheet of paper and smoothed it out on the table.

"Here you are, sir," said Mr. Hays, and pointed to an inscription —"Kelly's room." And then a cross: "Wife's jewels kept here."

Kelly looked and gasped. The cross marked exactly the place where in the daytime the jewellery was securely locked in a dressing-trunk.

"I said to myself," proceeded Mr. Hays, "'This man must be a burglar, and my job is to go along and warn the gentleman—'"

"What's he like?" asked Kelly, easily.

Mr. Hays's description was not very graphic. There were one or two points which left no doubt in the mind of Kelly who the burglar was. He made a few rapid inquiries. The cobbler lived alone in a small house on the outskirts of Finchley.

"He's out all night, is he?" said Kelly thoughtfully. "What about letting me in after he's gone one night?"

Mr. Hays hesitated and murmured something about the police.

"Never mind about the police, old boy," said Kelly, producing a convincing number of Treasury notes.

The next morning he gave his orders to his partner.

"You get back to Vienna by the first train and wait for me. I'll be returning in a day or two."

"What have you got on?" she asked, not unused to these sudden flits.

His answer was offensive.

That afternoon he paid his bill—his wife had already taken every bit of baggage and he could stroll forth unencumbered to the rendezvous.

He was not the only person who had received a visitor the night before. The brothers Pelcher were playing a peaceful game of dominoes in their ornate, over-decorated little drawing-room when the maid-of-all-work announced Mr. Hays.

"Hays? Who's Hays, Harry?" asked one of the other, but the information was not forthcoming.

Mr. Hays was a cobbler, a greyish man with a bristling moustache and a nervous manner. He had a small house in Finchley and a lodger....

"It's not for me, gentlemen, to put my nose into other people's affairs. I am a respectable, law-abiding citizen, as you gentlemen are. But I read the papers, and I got a headpiece that can put two and two together."

He paused, but the two silent men did no more than stare at him in their normally unfriendly manner.

"If you're not the two gentlemen who was knocked about one night some months ago, then I've made a mistake and I won't trouble you any further—I mean, two gentlemen named Pelcher... I read it in the papers. I keep a Press cutting book of things like that.

"It's a curious thing that this lodger of mine should have been looking over my shoulder as I was a-reading that bit about you two gentlemen being beaten up. 'Why do you keep that?' said he, laughing. When I told him I always pasted up horrors, he said: 'There's one thing they didn't tell the police—they didn't say anything about Henry Arthur Milton.'"

Both the brothers looked up quickly.

"Did he say any more?" asked Harry.

The cobbler fondled his unshaven chin.

"Yes, he did, sir, and that's why I've come to see you. He said: 'Those two fellers ought to have been settled, and one of these days I'm going down to have a look at them.'"

At their invitation, he described his lodger. The brothers looked at one another, and then Harry began to ask questions. When he was through with his inquiries he said to Hays: "If we gave you a couple of quid, what about going to the pictures tomorrow night and lending us the key of your house? You say he don't go out till ten?"

"Eleven," corrected Mr. Hays.

* * * *

For five pounds the cobbler surrendered the key. Kelly had paid twice that amount for the key's duplicate.

For the greater part of the night the brothers discussed possibilities. Said one:

"If we leave him in the house this old bird will put up a squeak. On the other hand, if we get in quiet and drop him somewhere, there will be no squeak at all, and nobody can swear that we went in."

There was agreement here. The second of the ferocious fraternity suggested knocking off a car. They found one the next night: a doctor's coupé, standing outside a house to which he had been called; and they drove cheerfully to the place of judgment.

It was a tiny house, with a tiny garden; and if the brothers had searched diligently in the untidy forecourt they would have discovered a board announcing that "this desirable residence" was to let.

This had been taken down by the cobbler when he had obtained possession of the premises a week before. He had apparently spent very little in furniture; for, although the passage had a narrow strip of carpet, the stairs were bare.

"The room at the head of the first flight of stairs," murmured one brother to the other before they inserted the key. "Have you got your rubbers on, Harry?"

Harry nodded. He had already covered his feet with snow boots.

They went in and closed the door noiselessly behind them. Harry went first up the stairs and paused by the closed door at the head. Somebody was inside. They heard a slight noise. Harry took out his life-preserver with a mirthless little grin, and gently turned the handle.

"Who's that?" said a voice from the dark interior.

The occupant of the room, unfortunately for himself, was silhouetted against the uncurtained window. Harry saw the gun with the bulging silencer at the end, and threw himself aside. There was a flash of light, a loud "plop!" and before the man with the pistol could shoot again the life-preserver got home.

* * * *

Two men got down from a car near Burlington Gardens, and each walked in a different direction. That, in itself, was a suspicious circumstance if it had been observed that at this hour—it was nearly ten—Burlington Gardens is more or less deserted save for cars that are taking a short cut to Regent Street.

146

A constable observed the machine, a closed car of American make, noted that the lights were on, and jotted down mentally the hour at which he saw it. When he returned from the perambulation of his beat the car was still there.

Burlington Gardens is not a parking place; there was no restaurant or hotel which might justify this "obstruction." He took the number and waited for the owners to reappear. He was relieved towards midnight and passed on the information and complaint to the officer who took his place.

At two o'clock the car had not been moved, and its occupants had not appeared. The only person who saw the two men was a night wanderer, an elderly vagrant, who subsequently gave information to the police.

At a little after three the sergeant to whom the matter was reported went up to the car and looked inside. In the light of his lamp he saw a motionless figure huddled on the floor, its head on its chest. He jerked open the door....

By the time the ambulance arrived they had laid the unfortunate man flat on the pavement. He was living—was to live for many years, though his appearance was never quite the same again.

The battered Kelly had a story to tell the police, and he spoke with difficulty.

"...two fellers...one of 'em was The Ringer!... He took my jewel-case from my hip-pocket...my watch and chain...about eighteen hundred quid ..."

The two brothers, who had separated in Burlington Gardens, met again at the corner of the street in which they dwelt. They had walked in single file within sight of one another until they were within easy reach of home, and then they joined up.

"I'm betting this feller doesn't use a cosh again for years."

"Is he dead, Harry?" asked his companion.

"It wasn't worth killing him," said Harry, complacently. "I want to have a look at that case as soon as we get indoors. I'll bet there are sparklers there worth thousands. And as for money..." His fingers closed on a thick wad of notes that he had neither counted nor examined.

They opened the door of their modest dwelling and walked into the drawing-room. Harry went first. "Clear!" he shouted.

Before the brothers could reach the door it was opened, and the front garden seemed more or less filled with constabulary.

* * * *

"Robbery with violence is one of the most serious offences that can be committed," said the Judge, in passing sentence upon the two dazed young men. "Your unfortunate victim is still in hospital, and, although he is a man of evil character, and one has the gravest doubts as to the origin of the property you stole, society must be protected. You will be kept in prison with hard labour for eighteen months, and will each receive twenty-five lashes with the cat-'o-nine-tails."

The extraordinary thing was that neither Kelly, the prosecutor, nor the brothers Pelcher ever mentioned the author of their misfortune.

Chapter 16

The Fortune Of Forgery

The man who reclined with his arms upon the parapet, looking down upon the dark water, was shabbily dressed. A "down-and-out," thought Henry Arthur Milton, smoking an after-dinner cigar, and promenading in the unexpected warmth of an early spring night along the Embankment.

He saw the man make a sudden jump upwards, gripped him by the arm, and swung him round.

"If you go into the water I shall have to jump in after you," said The Ringer pleasantly; "which means that I shall be very wet, very uncomfortable, and attract attention which I have no desire to attract."

The man was trembling from head to foot. His thin, unshaven face was gaunt and hollow. The shabby collar about his throat was frayed and ragged at the edges.

"I am very much obliged to you," he said.

It was the voice of an educated man, and his thanks were mechanical. He was obviously a gentleman; none but a gentleman would have received such a piece of unwarranted interference without resentment, without whining his troubles and his woes abroad.

"Come for a little walk," suggested The Ringer.

The man hesitated.

"I do not want any money," he said, "or charity of any kind."

The Ringer laughed softly.

"And I am not at all in a philanthropic mood," he replied.

He was, in truth, in a pretty bad temper. It was his peculiar complex and eccentricity that he hated reading letters to the editor in the daily newspapers abusing the police for their failure to arrest him. There had been three in a morning journal, and that which annoyed him most had been written by one Ferdinand Goldford, of Crake Hall, Bourne End.

The Ringer had his own views about coincidences. He regarded them as part of the normal processes of life. For example, if he picked up a tenfranc piece in the Strand he would expect to pick up a five-franc piece in the Lewisham High Road on the same day. He did not think such things were remarkable, and was only astounded when they did not happen.

149

The coincidence in this case was that he was very annoyed with Mr. Ferdinand Goldford, and that he should have rescued this human wreck from self-destruction.

"I think you ought to know," said the shabby man walking by his side, "that I was released from prison this morning, after serving two months for burgling a house in the country. I broke in to get what I thought was my own. The chief witness against me was the butler, who does not know me. The rest of the family are abroad."

"I hope they were having a good time," said The Ringer politely. "And as to your having been released from prison, believe me, I am so grateful that I have never been admitted into one that you may regard me as a spiritual complement."

The name of the wayfarer was Lopez Burt. He had once been an officer of a cavalry regiment in India. Mr. Milton was not surprised to learn this. He had been the heir-presumptive of a rich and eccentric father, whose eccentricities took serious shape while Burt was in India. He had left the whole of his fortune, no inconsiderable amount, to a cousin.

Lopez Burt might have contested the will, but he was not in a position, until months afterwards, to discover that his father had been "rather strange" in his manner for two years before his death, that he had lived with the fortunate cousin, and had made a new will at a period when he was quite incapable of any intellectual effort.

"I'm not kicking," he said philosophically.

"The poor old governor came a cropper on his head in the hunting field, and was never the same after that. The Goldfords kept this fact from me—"

"The who-fords?" asked The Ringer, immensely interested. "Not, by any chance, the Goldfords of Crake Hall, Bourne End?"

The man walking by his side nodded.

"That's the place I burgled," he said, almost cheerfully. "I came an awful mucker in the Army. You see, I got into debt, never dreaming but that I should have pots of money some day. Then there was some trouble over card debts, and I had to clear out.

"There was a lady in it, too," he added vaguely, "but I needn't mention her. Anyway, I landed in England with about fourpence-ha'penny, and after that...well, I hadn't any desire to see the Goldfords and throw myself upon their tender mercies. And I hadn't the evidence then about the governor being of unsound mind. Sounds like an old lag's story, doesn't it?"

The Ringer shook his head.

"It sounds remarkably unlike any old lag's story that I've heard," he said. "I have a top floor flat in the Adelphi. Will you come up and have a bite and a bath?"

150

"No," said the other, with emphasis.

The Ringer shook his head.

"Then I'm afraid I shall have to give you a punch on the nose," he remarked regretfully. "I am rather touchy on the subject of people refusing my invitations."

He heard the man chuckle.

"All right, I'll take your charity. I'm so hungry that I haven't any spirit left. My last meal was a piece of bread I scrounged from a garbage tin last night. That sounds picturesque, but it wasn't."

* * * *

The Ringer had a new furnished flat, which he had taken from a gentleman who had gone to Canada for a year: a pleasant, simply-furnished apartment, with hair carpets and stuff covers, and two or three cupboards containing valuables tightly locked—the usual "let."

"There is the bathroom." He threw open the door and switched on the light. "You had better eat something terrifically digestible. Try some sandwiches. I have a supply sent in to me every day."

He found a suit of clothes, a shirt, a collar, a pair of old shoes and the requisite etceteras, opened the bathroom door and threw them in on to the floor.

"Thank me when you come out, but don't be effusive," he said, and went out to hunt up sheets for the bed in the spare room.

At two o'clock in the morning The Ringer, who was a very good listener, came to the subject which was nearest his heart.

"These Goldbugs—Goldfords, is it?—seem to be a pretty unpleasant family."

He looked up at the ceiling thoughtfully and whistled.

"I suppose you've none of your former belongings? Have you any letters from your father?"

Lopez Burt looked at him quickly.

"Why do you ask that? Yes, I have quite a lot. They are in a box at my old Army bankers, with one or two other documents of no particular value."

The Ringer nodded.

"Is it possible to get those letters?"

Again Burt cast an odd look at his host.

"Will you tell me what the idea is?" he asked quietly.

Henry Arthur Milton stretched back in his chair and looked past him.

"I think I ought to tell you that I'm clairvoyant," he said. "Most of us are. The moment I saw you I had a feeling that you were the heir to a great fortune, and I naturally wondered why a man so favoured by the gods was contemplating such an early retirement from life."

"Great fortune!" scoffed the other. "What rot you're talking!"

The Ringer inclined his head graciously.

"That's one of my weaknesses," he said. "The truth is, I am talking rot! I have absolutely no knowledge in regard to the law affecting wills and such things. I presume that your cousins are now enjoying their ill-gotten gains and are rolling in wealth. How much money was there?"

"Seventy thousand pounds," said the other with a wry face. And then, with a shrug of his thick shoulders: "What does it matter?"

"How was the money left?" interrupted The Ringer.

"It had been left in equal parts to Mr. Ferdinand Goldford, Miss Lena Goldford, his sister, and Mr. Anthony Goldford, his brother. The funny thing about it was that the names were not specified.

* * * *

"The poor old governor simply wrote, 'To the children of my late brother-in-law, Tobias Goldford,' and that is where the dispute came in."

"Dispute?" said The Ringer quickly. "Was the will disputed?"

His visitor made a grimace of weariness.

"Don't let us talk about it."

"But I very much want to talk about it," said The Ringer. "Hasn't the will been made absolute, or whatever happens to these things?"

"Probate hasn't been granted—no. I thought of popping in, but a lawyer fellow I met on my tramp to London told me I hadn't a dog's chance. The trouble is that there's a fourth son by a former wife of Tobias, and in persuading the old man to make the will they'd forgotten all about him.

"He's been in South America and he claims to have a share. Old Tobias, by the way, was married the first time in South America and had this one son. There was a devil of a delay while they collected evidence. Naturally, the other Goldfords were furious with this fellow, and there have been all sorts of lawsuits—"

"Is Ferdinand Goldford a very offensive man?" asked The Ringer gently.

"He's an utter cad," was the prompt reply.

"I *am* clairvoyant," murmured Henry Arthur Milton, and a beatific smile dawned on his face.

Next morning The Ringer was early abroad pursuing his inquiries. He saw a copy of the will; it had been witnessed by two old servants of the deceased man, and was signed three months before his death. The Ringer returned from Somerset House primed with this information.

"Who was Jessica Brown and William Brown?" he asked.

"You mean the witnesses to the will?" Mr. Burt stopped in the middle of a very hearty breakfast to look up in some surprise. "You've been pretty early at the job!"

"Where are they to be found?"

"In Heaven," said Lopez Burt grimly. "They only survived the poor governor by about five months. My lawyer pal—by the way, I met him in prison again—told me that there might be a chance of upsetting the will if they were alive. They were a nice old couple. They used to write to me regularly in India. They knew me when I was a child. I suppose I've dozens of their letters—"

"Are they in the box, too?" asked The Ringer quickly.

Lopez Burt considered.

"Yes; I don't think there is anything but letters."

"Splendid!" said his host. "This morning you will go along and collect that box and bring it here."

* * * *

A week later a smart-looking man of middle age, with an iron-grey moustache, alighted from an expensive motorcar before the porch of Crake Hall, and the florid Ferdinand, who had been playing clock golf on the lawn, loafed across to discover the identity of the visitor.

"Good-morning," said the caller brusquely. "I'm Colonel St. Vinnes. Is Burt anywhere about?"

"Burt?" said Ferdie in amazement. "Do you mean my cousin, Lopez Burt? Good Lord! I thought everybody knew about him. He got into serious trouble in India and had to clear out—"

"I know, I know," snapped the other. "But that was before the Lal Singh affair—the lucky young devil! If he wastes that fortune I'll never forgive him. I thought he had come back from America—"

Ferdinand Goldford was very much interested. Money fascinated him.

"Is that old Lope you're talking about?" he asked, not concealing his astonishment. "Got a lot of money, has he? We haven't heard from him."

The Colonel's face expressed astonishment.

"He's not here, then? Dear, dear, dear, that's extremely awkward!"

Ferdinand was impressed.

"Won't you come in?" he invited, and the visitor followed him through the large square hall into the drawing-room, and found himself being introduced to Ferdie's brother and sister—florid replicas of Ferdie, with the same fresh, round faces and small, blue eyes. Mr. Burt had described them as "pig-cunning," and this was not an inapt description.

"Friend of old Lope's," said Ferdinand loudly, as though he were prepared in advance to drown their protests. "Colonel—um—"

The visitor supplied his name.

"Old Lope's made a lot of money...in America now."

Mr. Goldford spoke rapidly. They eyed the visitor suspiciously, incredulously. Apparently the idea of Lope making money was a paralysing one.

"The point is," said the Colonel, looking at his watch, "how can I get in touch with him? I had a cable saying that he would call here in the course of the day, but I've got to go back to London. Is it possible for me to leave a letter for him?"

It was not only possible, but Ferdie was most anxious to facilitate the process.

"Come this way, Colonel."

They passed down a broad passage into a lovely old room, the walls covered with bookshelves.

"This was the old fellow's library. We don't use it much now. Here's a table; there is no ink, but perhaps you'd like to use my fountain-pen?"

The Colonel had a pen of his own. Ferdie bustled out to get the necessary stationery. He came back in a few minutes and explained that this room was seldom used.

"Too many books, too smelly, too dismal," he said, as he laid the paper before the visitor. "We can't clear it out till this will business is settled. That ought to happen in a couple of weeks."

"It seems rather a nice library," said the Colonel, glancing round.

Ferdie smiled.

"Don't you believe it! There isn't a book here worth reading. Look at 'em."

Certainly the bookshelves had a very solid appearance. There was one filled with ancient tomes, the covers of which were considerably dilapidated.

The Colonel wrote his letter, with Mr. Goldford standing over him. He had sharp eyes and could read "My dear Lope" and "terribly sorry I missed you…" but he really wasn't trying hard to discover the contents of the letter. That could easily be steamed open after this military-looking gentleman had left. Indeed, the Colonel was hardly out of the grounds before the family were perusing the four-page letter that he had written.

"Nothing—absolutely nothing," said Ferdinand, and his brother agreed.

Certain shares were referred to, but not specifically mentioned. Ferdie re-sealed the letter and put it aside for his cousin when he called.

* * * *

"What do I do now?" asked Lopez Burt when The Ringer joined him at dinner that night in his little Adelphi flat. "You will emulate the rabbit who laid low, and maintain a discreet silence," said Henry Arthur Milton. "I am thoroughly enjoying this little adventure. You went to the tailor's?"

Lope nodded.

"It wasn't as ghastly as I thought," he replied, "and I'm getting almost used to ready-made clothes. They didn't fit me very well in prison. They're making a few alterations and delivering them tonight. I suppose you realise I have already spent over a hundred pounds of your money?"

"You will spend more," said The Ringer cheerfully. "As soon as your clothes arrive you will pack them, take a taxi and drive to the *Ritz-Carlton*. I've already reserved your room in advance. When you get there you will write to your lawyer, Mr. Stenning—Stenning and Stenning, isn't it?

"You will say that you have arrived, and you'll be glad if he will come to dinner one night. He won't come, because he's one of those old gentlemen who never go out. I have written to him already."

"You've written to him?" said the other incredulously. "Why?"

"You promised to ask no questions," said The Ringer, with one of his rare smiles. "All I want you to do is to establish the fact that you're living in luxury somewhere in London."

Lopez Burt shook his head in bewilderment.

"I don't know what the idea is—" he began.

"Don't try. All you have to do is to sit tight and wait for good fortune," said The Ringer. "I didn't like Mr. Goldford before I saw him. Why, I cannot explain. When I saw him I loathed him. I made a few inquiries—some tradesmen are very talkative—and there's no doubt that these people descended on your unfortunate father at a period when he was unable to resist their influence.

"He was not staying with them, as you supposed. They were staying with him. It is an extraordinary piece of good luck that they are constantly dismissing and engaging servants."

"Where's the luck in that?"

But The Ringer did not explain.

"Another bit of good luck," he went on, "was that there was no stationery in the library. If there had been I should have taken another course."

"I'm not going to ask any more questions," said Lopez Burt. "You've been a brick to me, and if ever I can repay you—"

"Not only can you repay me, but you will. I'm trusting you to say nothing about myself. Here is an address in Berlin: I want you to keep that by you and never lose it. As soon as you're in a position to do so you can send me £6,000, which I shall regard as commission well earned."

Lopez Burt smiled.

"You'll have to wait a very long time for that!" he said.

"Not so long," said The Ringer cryptically.

* * * *

That morning, Mr. Samuel Stenning, the senior partner of Stenning and Stenning, received a letter. It was addressed to him personally, expressed, and certain words in the ill-written and illiterate communication were heavily underlined.

...I could tell you things that are going on at old Mr. Burt's place that would make your hare stand up on end! I know what happened before he died, when he sent for old Mr. Brown and had a long talk with him...he wasn't daft then.

He came down to the libery and I see him put something in a book. It was on the third shelf, it was called "Concrudence." I often wanted to look and see what it was, but I never had a chants.

I'll bet it was something about the Goldfords, who are a miserable lot of people and don't deserve to live in the house of a gentleman. I'll bet this thing he put in the Concrudence was a showing up for the Goldfords.

The letter bore the signature "A Friend." Mr. Stenning was not unused to anonymous letters, and ordinarily would have dropped it in the wastepaper basket; but he, too, disliked the Goldfords exceedingly, and had been secretly pleased when a new heir had appeared on the scene and had disputed their share of their ill-won possessions.

Unfortunately he had been a semi-invalid in the south of France when the will was made, and had no knowledge of its circumstances; but he was satisfied in his own mind that old man Burt was not in a condition to dispose of his property, and if he had had the slightest evidence on which the will could have been opposed he would have combed the earth for Mr. Burt's unfortunate son.

It was a remarkable coincidence that that morning he should receive a note from the *Ritz-Carlton* announcing the arrival of Lopez Burt in London.

"Humph!" said Mr. Stenning. "That's queer!"

He turned the matter over in his mind all day, and the following morning, instead of going to the office, he and his clerk went down in his car to Bourne End. Mr. Goldford was not so surprised to see him as he had imagined he would be.

"Good-morning, Mr. Stenning. Have you seen anything of Lope?"

"I believe he is in London," said Stenning, himself astonished. "Did you know?"

Ferdinand grinned.

"No, I haven't heard from him. Somebody called here for him yesterday and left a note. You might give it to him if you see him. Is anything wrong?"

"No; I've had some information on which I feel compelled to act," said Mr. Stenning. "Have you found any documents belonging to your uncle?"

A look of alarm came to the round face of Ferdie.

"Documents?" he squeaked. "No—what documents could there be?"

"Has the place been searched thoroughly?"

"We've had his desk and boxes opened, and most of the letters he left behind were sent to your office," said Ferdinand. "There has been nothing else. What do you expect?"

"Can I look in the library?"

Ferdinand hesitated.

"Certainly," he said.

He went in first and must have communicated the news to his brother and sister, for when Mr. Stenning and his clerk reached the drawing-room their reception was a chilly one.

"What's the idea of all this nonsense?" asked Ferdinand irritably. "What documents could he have left? I know you don't think he was in his right mind, but there's the will, signed and witnessed—"

"By two people who are now dead," said Stenning drily.

Ferdinand's face flushed an angry red.

"That doesn't invalidate the will, does it?" he demanded angrily. "Of course they're dead. You saw them when they were alive; didn't they tell you that Mr. Burt was perfectly normal...?"

"What's the use of arguing, Ferdie?" said the shrill voice of his sister. "Let's go in and see the library."

The lawyer and his clerk accompanied the family into the gloomy room. Stenning walked up and down, examining the books on the third shelf. Presently his hand went up. It was Cruden's Concordance.

"I am informed there is something here," he said.

He took down the book, laid it on the table, and it opened on a faded sheet of paper. Ferdie saw the heading, gasped, and his jaw dropped.

"Good God!" he said.

It was headed "The Last Will and Testament," and was written in the crabbed hand of old Mr. Burt. The lawyer read the document carefully. It revoked all former wills, and "particularly the will I made on the seventeenth of February last, and which I now regard as being neither just nor equitable," and left the whole of his property to Lopez Henry Martin Burt, "my dear son."

The signature was undoubtedly that of the dead man. Beyond any question the witnesses were those who had witnessed the other will—and it had been made three weeks later!

"I'll dispute this," stormed Ferdinand, pale and quavering. "The thing's a forgery—there are no witnesses—"

"The same people witnessed the will in your favour," said the lawyer with quiet malice. "I am afraid this document will make a great difference to you."

He put the will in his pocket. For a second Ferdie's attitude suggested that he would take it from him by force.

"It's a forgery!" he bellowed. "I'll dispute it, by God! if I have to spend every penny...."

"You haven't many pennies to spend of your own, Mr. Goldford," said the lawyer acidly.

* * * *

Seven months later Lopez Burt enclosed an open draft for six thousand pounds in a letter he posted to an address in Berlin. He wrote:

> I don't know exactly how it all happened, but the Court have upheld my claim. I am still mystified as to how you knew of the other will—that is the greatest puzzle of all.
>
> The document was undoubtedly in my father's handwriting, and I could swear to the signatures of the two witnesses....
>
> Do you remember asking me to get the box from the bank? You must have seen a lot of my father's writing there, and also the letters from the two servants.
>
> If you'd seen the will also you would have agreed that there was no question as to the authenticity of the document.

The Ringer purred at this. He was rather proud of his draughtsmanship, and he had reason to be. He had forged that will in four hours, which was something of an achievement.

Chapter 17

A "Yard" Man Kidnapped

Government Departments keep a sharp eye on post-prandial oratory. They do not like their servants, high or low, to talk shop in their leisure hours. Certainly they strongly discount anything that has the appearance of being criticism of superiors; and Inspector Mander overstepped the bounds when, at a police banquet, and in the course of proposing such an innocuous toast as "The Ladies," he made a reference to The Ringer.

"People sometimes criticise us because notorious criminals remain at large," he said. (The quotation is from the *Outer London News and Suburban Record*.) "I am not so sure that we have done all we might have done, or that the right methods have been employed to bring him under arrest. This man is not only a menace to society, but a mark of reproach against our administration."

If Bliss had not disliked him so intensely, he would have broken Inspector Mander. It was the knowledge that he actively loathed this cocksure officer that induced him to excuse his error. Nevertheless, Inspector Mander stepped upon the carpet before a very high official and spent a most uncomfortable ten minutes, during which he did most of the listening.

It was three days after the publication of Mander's speech in a weekly newspaper that Bliss received a letter from The Ringer.

> I am rather tired of Mander, and I think I will put him where he belongs. Fools rather terrify me because they have the assistance of Providence—which is distinctly unfair.
>
> You may tell Mr. Mander from me that before the end of the week has passed I shall get him.

Bliss sent for his subordinate.

"Read this," he said.

Mander read and forced a smile, but the superintendent knew that he was none too happy.

"He has never threatened you before, has he?" asked Bliss.

Mander laughed, but there was no real mirth in it.

"That kind of bunk doesn't scare me," he said. "I've been threatened by
—"

"By The Ringer?" asked Bliss maliciously, enjoying the officer's dis-
comfiture.

Mander moved uneasily in his chair.

"Well, no, not by The Ringer, but—er—I don't take very much notice of
that."

And then he brightened visibly.

"You can see, chief, that this fellow's scared of me, and—"

"Excuse me a moment while I laugh," said Bliss sardonically. "Scared of
you! What job are you on now?"

Mr. Mander was dealing with a case of car-stealing. He had got on the
track of a fairly important organisation which, if it did not actually steal,
certainly played the part of a receiver. Bliss listened and nodded.

"You ought to be safe," he said. "You've got Sergeant Crampton working with you; he's a pretty intelligent man."

Mander winced.

"The Duke of Kyle—" he began, and the nose of Mr. Bliss wrinkled.

"The Duke of Kyle is a great authority on the breeding of pigs and nothing else—oh, yes, I read his letter in the *Monitor*, praising your speech.
That nearly got you hung. But he's no authority on The Ringer."

The Duke of Kyle was one of those peers who had very little occupation
in life other than the breeding of pigs and the inditing of letters to newspapers. He had written his unqualified approval of Mr. Mander's speech, and
had, moreover, suggested fantastical and not even novel methods for bringing The Ringer to justice. Bliss had read and had feared for his Grace.

* * * *

That night Mander was at Netting Dale Police Station, pursuing his inquiries, and was coming down the steps when a beautiful limousine drew
up at the door and a lady in evening dress stepped down. She was fair-
haired and very beautiful; her hands sparkled with diamonds; from her ears
hung two glittering stones.

"Can you tell me where I can find Inspector Mander?" she asked, and
Mander, susceptible to feminine charms, lifted his hat. "You're he? Mr.
Bliss said I should find you here."

"Is anything wrong, madam?"

The lady nodded; she seemed a little breathless, considerably agitated.

"It is about my car," she said, lowering her voice, "a coupé. It was stolen
this afternoon while I was shopping in Bond Street. Somebody enticed the
chauffeur away.... It isn't the loss of the car. I wonder if I could speak to
you alone? Could you come back to Berkeley Square with me?"

Mander gave instructions to his men and followed the lady into the luxurious, delicately-perfumed interior. She was silent for a while.

"It isn't the loss of the car," she said again, "but I foolishly left my handbag in the pocket. There are letters there—it's very difficult to tell you this—that I—I wish to recover. I can speak to you confidentially?"

"Certainly, madam," said Mander.

His proximity to such a fragrant, lovely being was a little intoxicating.

"The Duke and I are not on very good terms, but there has never been a question of—divorce. These letters will make a tremendous difference to me. Is it true that such things can be recovered through the—the underworld?"

Mander smiled.

"They say so in books, and it has happened in real life," he said, "but it has never been my experience."

If Inspector Mander had been a little more experienced he would have returned a different answer.

"They're compromising letters, I suppose?"

"Compromising? Yes—well, I suppose they are. They're from a boy—my cousin. Oh, dear, oh, dear!" She wrung her hands in despair.

"I'll try to get them for your Grace," said Mander gallantly.

He did not know which duchess this was. His acquaintance with the peerage was slight and sketchy, and the only member he knew was an impoverished lord who occasionally found himself on the verge of prosecution.

She opened a little flap in the car before her and took out a jewelled cigarette case—in that half-light the diamond monogram sparkled brilliantly.

"Do smoke."

He took a cigarette and politely offered her a light to the cigarette she put between her red lips. There was a little microphone attachment at the side of the car, and she pressed a button. Mander saw the chauffeur bend his head towards the earpiece.

"Drive round the park for a little while before you go to Berkeley Square," she commanded.

In the light of his match Mander had seen the ducal coronet and a "K." The Duchess of——? Kyle, of course!

"The trouble with Bertie is that he's very indiscreet," she said. "He writes letters…."

Mander, who had settled himself more comfortably in the corner of the car, most unaccountably fell asleep at this juncture.

* * * *

161

The ringing of the telephone bell brought Bliss from his bed and into the cold room where the instrument was. Detectives are human, and they never quite get accustomed to being wakened at half-past three in the morning.

"Mander? What do I know about Mander? Why? Ring him up, my dear man," he said testily.

"He's not in his house, sir. We haven't seen him since he went away with the lady."

Bliss was instantly wide awake.

"Which lady?"

The man at the other end of the phone told him of the car that called at Notting Dale.

"It's the Duke of Kyle's car," said that same Sergeant Crampton in whose intelligence Bliss had expressed his unbounded faith. "We found it abandoned on Hampstead Heath. It had been stolen from his Grace's garage."

"Have you searched it?"

"Yes, sir. We found rather an important clue—a lady's card, with a few words scribbled in pencil."

"Bring the car round and pick me up," said Bliss, and was waiting in the street before the police tender came in sight.

By the light of the headlamps he examined the card. In a woman's hand was written:

The Leek. First left, first right.—Stillman.

"Now, look at this, sir," said the sergeant.

He switched on the lights inside the car, which was upholstered in fawn. The tiny carpet on the floor was of the same colour, but near the left-hand door was a large red patch, and on the padded upholstery on the near side of the car a larger patch level with a man's head.

"It's blood," said the sergeant. "I saw him go off, and that's the seat he occupied."

The local inspector of police was present at the examination.

"What is The Leek? Is there such a place near here?"

The inspector shook his head.

"No, but Stillman is the name of a house agent. He lives in Shardeloes Road. I've sent one of my men to wake him. He ought to be up by now: will you come round?"

They drove round to Shardeloes Road and found a sleepy, middle-aged man.

"The Leek is a cottage—I always call it The Leek; that was the former name of it. It's an empty house on the edge of the heath."

He took the card, examined it, and nodded.

"That's right. A lady asked to see it and I gave her the directions. That's the handwriting of my clerk."

"Have you the keys of this place?"

"Yes, at my office. If you wait, I'll dress."

* * * *

They waited while he dressed, accompanied him to his office in the steep hill street, and, crossing the heath, dipped into a depression. The road ran for some distance through an avenue of trees, at the end of which were three or four houses. Mr. Stillman stopped the car at the first of these, and the detectives jumped out.

It was a gloomy-looking little house with a forecourt behind the high wall. They passed into the garden through a wicket gate, and Sergeant Crampton, using his lamp, led the way. Presently he stopped.

"Look at this," he said.

On the stone flags were certain red stains, which were still wet. A little farther along were others. When they reached the door they found it half open.

Bliss went ahead with Crampton into the musty-smelling house, his lamp searching the walls carefully. There was blood on the floor, blood on the walls; the trail led him upward to the front room.

Here the evidence of tragedy was almost complete. There were bloodstains everywhere, but if there was no sign of the body there was evidence of a struggle, for one of the walls was spattered red, and near the door he found the sanguinary print of a gloved hand.

He made a careful scrutiny of every room, but apparently only the front room had been visited by Mander and his captor.

At four o'clock they were coming out of the house, when a car drove up and a man stepped out. Crampton went to interview him, and returned with the information that it was the Duke of Kyle's secretary.

"I had to telegraph to his Grace about the car being stolen," he said. "His Grace is very much upset. The Ringer visited him last night."

"Where?" asked Bliss quickly.

"At Clane Farm—it is near Sevenoaks. His lordship has a large pig-breeding establishment there," said this middle-aged gentleman.

Apparently the Duke had been retiring for the night, when somebody had tapped on the window of his study; he had drawn up the window and seen a strange and, to him, a terrifying face.

"He was armed," said the secretary, his voice quaking. "He made the most terrible threats to his Grace. He said he was bringing a Mr. Mander to stay with him that night, and that they would both be found in the same condition in the morning."

163

"Did he notify the police?" asked Bliss.

"No, sir." The secretary shook his head. "His Grace is a very courageous man. It was very curious that I should have been getting on to him at the moment that he was trying to get into communication with me. He told me he was sitting up all night, and that he would be heavily armed."

Bliss noted down the exact location of the pig farm.

"Can you get on to his Grace and tell him that we're coming down almost immediately?" he asked. "I want to make an examination of this road."

After Mr. Whistle—for such was his peculiar name—had departed the detective began a systematic search for further clues.

The path outside was of gravel, and, although there were stains which had the appearance of blood, they were not sufficiently definite or informative to help very much. Fifty yards along the road, however, Bliss made a discovery. It was a large piece of bloodstained satin, rolled up and thrown on one side. From here the evidences of tragedy were clear to the naked eye. They followed the track of the tell-tale spots across the Heath until they came to the edge of a pond, where they had ceased.

Bliss observed that the pond was within easy walking distance of the place where the car had been found, and this puzzled him. If Mander had been killed, why had not the body been immediately disposed of? Why had it been taken to the house?

This was not the only thing that puzzled him. The detectives probed into the water with their sticks, but at the place where the track ceased the water was deep. Bliss gave instructions that the pond was to be dragged, but did not wait to see the result.

* * * *

Ten minutes later the police car was speeding across Westminster Bridge on its southward journey.

Daylight broke before they reached Clane Farm. It was rather a difficult place to locate, and Bliss regretted that he had not brought the secretary with him. They found it at last and saw that there were strange activities, for in the narrow lane they met three men beating the hedges and obviously searching for something. Bliss stopped the car and was addressed by the red-faced leader:

"Are you the police?" he demanded. "That's quick work. I only telephoned you a quarter of an hour ago."

"I'm from Scotland Yard," said Bliss. "What's the trouble?"

"Trouble?" roared the man, going red in the face. "Pride of Kent's been stolen. He couldn't have got out of his pen—"

"Who's Pride of Kent?"

"The finest hog in the country," said the man. "He's taken every first prize, and I wouldn't have lost him for a thousand pounds. When his Grace hears about it there's going to be trouble."

"When was he lost?"

"Last night. He was in his sty, and he couldn't have got out by himself," said the man. "One of these villagers must have come up and stolen him. If we catch him there's going to be trouble. I wouldn't be surprised if he'd been killed. You found blood, didn't you, Harry?"

"Yes, sir, I found blood," said the man he addressed. "It were near the old building."

"Where is his Grace?" asked Bliss.

The man stared at him.

"His Grace? Why, he's in Scotland."

The eyes of Mr. Bliss opened.

"In Scotland? Are you sure?"

"Yes, I'm sure," said the man impatiently. "I had a letter from his Grace yesterday. At least, not from his Grace, but from his secretary, Miss Erford."

Superintendent Bliss did not so much as wince.

"Is there a Mr. Whistle?"

The man had never heard of Mr. Whistle.

* * * *

Bliss regretted even more that he had not brought the "secretary" with him, though he had no doubt that that gentleman would have found a very excellent excuse for remaining in London.

"There are lots of people who didn't like Pride of Kent," the man proceeded. "Some of these pigmen had a grudge against him because he was a bit savage; but he was the best hog in the county, and I don't know what his Grace will say if I can't find him."

"Where was this pig kept?" asked Bliss.

The Pride of Kent lived in a handsome mansion which many of his Grace's tenants might have envied. It was a low building, before which was an ample yard, where the joy of the piggery could rest at his well-fed ease. A steel grating was unfastened and the pigman explained just how impossible it was for anybody but an educated porker to let himself out.

"My theory is that it happened last night," said the man. "There was a van seen in the lane—"

"What is this?" said Bliss, and, stooping, picked up a round tin. It was half-filled with a brown, treacly substance. "Have you seen this before?"

The foreman shook his head. There was a small label on the tin, a wafer of paper, and on this was written the word "Poison."

"The Ringer is about the most thoughtful man I have ever met with," said Bliss bitterly, for he recognised the queer "n" that Henry Arthur Milton invariably made. "We'll have that for analysis," he said. "I suppose the Pride of Kent was rather fond of sweet things? I thought so. This looks to me like golden syrup—and something else! I can well understand why he didn't put up a squeak."

The pigman did not see the grim jest. "What is that over there?" asked Bliss. He pointed to a range of buildings, each with its little front forecourt.

"We keep the young pigs there. They are his last litter," said the pigman proudly. "You won't find a better lot in Kent or anywhere else."

The forecourts were filled with little porkers, all engaged at that moment in their morning meal. At the second pen Mr. Bliss paused. In one corner was a round felt hat sadly battered and slightly gnawed.

"I think I'd like to go in here," said Bliss, and stepped in among the terrified little pigs, who scampered in all directions save one—this was significant. They did not go into the dark little house where they slept at night. One or two did approach the entrance, but turned and fled instantly.

* * * *

Bliss stooped low and passed through the door. The man who sat propped up in one corner bound hand and foot and scientifically gagged stared pathetically into the eyes of his chief.

"Come in here," called Bliss, and the two detectives who were with him followed.

It took them some little time to unfasten his bonds, but presently Mr. Mander staggered out into the light and was stimulated with brandy.

He had nothing to say; he could only babble about a beautiful lady, and somebody who carried him on his back. His most distinct recollection was facing the tiny eyes of a dozen little pigs, who resented his intrusion into their sleeping quarters.

"Queer, isn't it?" said Bliss absently. "He said he'd put you where you belonged. I won't be so uncomplimentary as to say that he did."

"This woman was one of the prettiest—"

"I have met Cora Ann Milton before, but I didn't know she was in England," said Bliss; "and I don't suppose she is this morning."

One of the servants of the house came hurrying towards him.

"There's a telephone message for you, sir—"

Bliss waved him aside.

"I know all about it. They've found the body of the Pride of Kent in the pond at Hampstead. I know exactly where the bloodstains came from. I'm pretty sure I know where that unfortunate hog was killed."

* 9 7 8 1 6 6 7 6 8 3 1 0 2 *